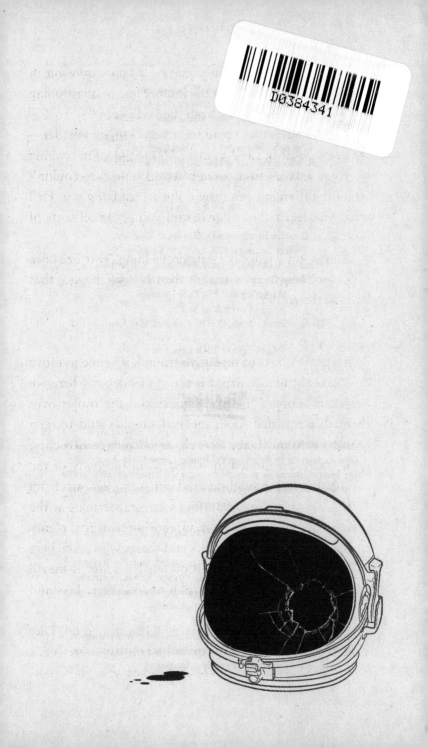

An Abaddon Books™ Publication
www.abaddonbooks.com
abaddon@rebellion.co.uk

First published in 2018 by Abaddon Books™,
Rebellion Publishing Limited, Riverside House,
Osney Mead, Oxford, OX2 0ES, UK.

10 9 8 7 6 5 4 3 2 1

Creative Director and CEO: Jason Kingsley
Chief Technical Officer: Chris Kingsley
Head of Books and Comics Publishing: Ben Smith
Fiction Commissioning Editor: David Moore
Marketing and PR: Remy Njambi
Cover: Maz Smith
Design: Sam Gretton, Oz Osborne and Maz Smith

Copyright © 2018 Rebellion.
All rights reserved.

Abaddon Books and Abaddon Books logo are trademarks owned or
used exclusively by Rebellion Publishing Limited. The trademarks
have been registered or protection sought in all member states of the
European Union and other countries around the world. All rights
reserved.

ISBN: 978-1-78108-634-6

No part of this publication may be reproduced, stored in a retrieval
system, or transmitted in any form or by any means, electronic,
mechanical, photocopying, recording or otherwise, without the prior
permission of the publishers.

This is a work of fiction. All the characters and events portrayed
in this book are fictional, and any resemblance to real people or
incidents is purely coincidental.

DEATH OF A CLONE

ALEX THOMSON

ABADDON
BOOKS

For Nicki

HELL

1

HELL

THE ASTEROID'S OFFICIAL name is Mizushima-00109, but all of us know it simply as 'Hell.' One of the Overseers must have called it that once, as a joke, and it stuck. I can't remember ever knowing what the word meant— it was just the word for the black chunk of rock and metal where we lived, used in everyday speech, as in "Has anyone ever mapped out Hell's south-western ridge?"

Then one cycle, I was reading one of Mr Lee's books—a Dickens, I think—and the word cropped up, and I had to ask him to explain to me what Hell was. He says the Overseer who first called the asteroid Hell was being ironical, but I don't buy it. Us, the Overseers can bear.

And the work is tolerable for them—a distraction. But Mizushima-00109 itself… they really, really, *viscerally* hate it. A big, dumb, pitiless lump of metal. Its toxic atmosphere, its pale sun. You can see why they hate it— for them, it's a constant reminder of where they are not: Earth. For the rest of us, though—the Ays, the Bees, the Jays and we two poor Ells, it's all we've ever known.

Hell. Home.

I STARE OUT the cabin window, and watch as time creeps imperceptibly past. The others, they can't do this, they have to fill their time somehow. Like the Ays, pacing up and down along the tunnels, shadowboxing, muttering— or the Jays, with their chess marathons. Even Lily, my sister, she gets bored eventually. But I can do this for hours, just sit and stare and empty my mind.

I'M OFTEN ALONE here—with only two of us, it's unusual for both of us to be on a Leisure shift at the same time. The cabin is designed for six—so the extra space has become a communal dumping ground for broken machinery and rubbish. All in all, we have the same amount of personal space as the others; which is to say, not a lot. The Overseers each have their own cabin, but you wouldn't know it, listening to their gripes. Not that I begrudge them their space—I wouldn't know what to do with it all.

Outside, the stars inch infinitesimally further to the

right. There is a particularly bright one, which is surely not a star but Mars, six light minutes away. And one of them, somewhere among the multitude, must be Earth.

Just a few cycles ago, I was in the Leisure cabin while Mr Reynolds gave an astronomy lecture to anyone who would listen. He was pointing towards the window covering the wall, identifying various constellations, when his finger stopped dead.

"There," he said. "Earth. I'd know it anywhere."

I couldn't see where he was pointing, and in any case, I'm sure he had no clue what he was talking about. Of the three remaining Overseers, he's the one who misses the comforts of Earth the most. Even when he's out on the surface of Hell, he's like a caged animal, glowering, kicking out at stray chunks of ore. And I've heard him before, saying he should never have come here, he made the wrong choice. But Mr Ortiz stared at him and he shut up.

As for me, I will miss Hell when the Collection Ship comes, in around six hundred cycles. Something about the way it's so magnificently indifferent to us, and our work here. So self-contained—you could walk the entire circumference, if you were so inclined and had a limitless air supply, in a dozen cycles. Two and a half orbits we've been here, six Earth years of life. But it never gets old— it'll always be home.

Earth, though... some of the brothers and sisters— especially the Bees—can't wait, they spend hours of dull conversation about what they're going to do there. But Earth terrifies me. Even after millennia of living there, we still don't understand it, can't control it, can't survive on great swathes of its surface. What have we been doing all this time?

Mr Lee says I worry too much.

A rustle startles me and I glance over to where Lily is stirring. She pushes her sheets aside and sits on the bunk. My own boggy morning face stares back at me.

"So," she says.

"So," I reply.

She grabs a grey boiler suit and pulls it on, up to her waist. "I have a work shift commencing in one hour and twelve minutes," she says, looking up at the clock.

"I have a sleep shift commencing in one hour and twelve minutes," I say. Sometimes we play a game, to see who can be the most boring—if you quit the conversation or say something original, you lose. But this cycle, I can tell she's not in the mood. She slumps back down on the bunk, and I go to sit behind her. I lift up her nightshirt and start to tickle her back. It helps her to wake up. Both of us have our eyes on the Earth clock—irrelevant to the short cycles of Hell, but as good a way as any of measuring time, and it gives a vague comfort to the Overseers. I note the time—when our situations are reversed, I will get the exact amount of back-tickling time in return.

"Leila," she says, "my head hurts. I mean, it really hurts."

I don't respond. The headaches are part of life.

"Why don't the Overseers' heads hurt like this?" she says. "Why just us?"

"Could just be the pills they take. Or maybe they do feel it, but they just have a different pain threshold."

"Oh, sure, you think they wouldn't make a fuss?"

"I mean, they might just feel it differently. It's like… if you put your fingers in your ears, noise is all muffled, right? But the noise is still there."

"So?"

"So it could be the same with pain. The pain's there, it just depends how you perceive it."

Lily twists round and stares at me. "Leila?"

"Yes?"

"Shut up and tickle."

I shut up and tickle. After a bit I say, "Who else will be on your work shift?"

"Do you care?" she replies. "Juan? Judas? Jupiter? Does it matter?"

She is enjoying the tickle. I can feel her back relaxing and loosening its knots.

"Just making conversation," I say brightly, which is what she says to me when I moan. In some of the books I've read, twins have a kind of telepathic understanding—they don't need to say the mundane stuff, it's all unspoken and understood. Lily and I, we don't have that, we're always having misunderstandings and asking each other to spell out exactly what we mean.

With one hand I knead her shoulder blades, and she purrs with pleasure. This will all be paid back to me. There is silence for a few minutes while I work on her.

"Leila," she says, eyes closed. "What do you think happened to our sisters, really?"

According to Mr Lee, our four sisters did not grow properly. Out on the ship, in the vats, some piece of machinery had failed during the process—or perhaps it was human error. Nobody seemed to know. They were never even named.

"What do you mean, 'really'?" I ask.

"I was talking to Mr Lee about it—I swear he doesn't have a clue what happened. He gets all vague, tries to change the subject."

"He probably doesn't understand—he's not a scientist, is he?"

Lily gives an exasperated sigh. "It doesn't make sense, Lei. I can believe an accident happened. But why send down just two Ells? They must have had more Ells on the ship—or at least four more of another similar Family."

"So?"

"So he's lying about what happened. Why would they allow this to disrupt the whole group dynamic, and mess up our work timetable? Nobody benefits."

In one sense, she was right—the work was disrupted: Ells were responsible for transportation of ore from the excavation sites back to the depots, and the categorisation of the ore. But with just two of us, much of that work had to be offloaded onto the others, who found it hard enough just to keep up with their quotas. And yes, the group dynamic had been skewed—hundreds of hours had been spent testing and theorising to come up with the best combinations to send to the different asteroids. For Mizushima-00109, that was six Ays, six Bees, six Jays and six Ells. You don't have to be a genius to realise that missing four Ells would blow those theories out the water.

But, despite all this, Lily had failed to take into account the difference between theory and practice. Reading books had prepared me for this—the messy gulf between what *should* be, and the eventual compromise. Lily imagined chrome vats on a humming spaceship, production lines churning out brothers and sisters, supervisors directing them this way and that with prim efficiency. Me, I saw the flickering light bulb, the boredom, the unspoken sense of *This'll have to do.*

Fiction. I swear, it turns you into a cynic.

"It was just a cock-up," I say. "Mistakes happen."

I feel like I've had this conversation before, word for word. Though it could just as easily be a conversation I've had with myself, in my head.

"I'm going to get to the bottom of it," she says, like I knew she would, for we are stubborn if nothing else. "Something stinks here, Lei, you know it does."

"Well, good luck with that. I'm just not sure what you think you'll find on Hell."

"I'm not saying it's going to be easy, but I've got to try, for our sisters. Just like if something happened to me, you'd look out for me."

"Yeah, well."

Lily wriggles and arches her back, trying to direct my fingers to the most ticklish spot. "That's it... right... there." A pause. "I wish we were like the other families, Lei. You know, a six."

I sniff. "I like it, the two of us. Lil and Lei."

"Poor Jays, though," she says.

This is a long-running source of controversy on Hell. Jays and Ells were always intended as sexual partners, but how does six divide into two? The Ays and Bees have always paired off as planned, with no difficulties. Even when Avery died last orbit, a tunnel collapsing on him, the dynamic survived. Six can, just about, go into five. Especially when you have identical sisters. Lily is desperate to know the practicalities of how they manage it, but was too shy to ask one of the Bees; and now the moment has passed.

The Jays and Ells, though—that's caused a lot of argument and gossip, in a small community like ours. Mr Lee fought our corner: he has always been brutally, unquestioningly loyal. He would never allow for the two of us to be passed around between the six Jays like some kind of inverted harem. And equally, it would never work for us both to choose one Jay and pair off exclusively with them; it would twist the dynamic beyond breaking point. So we co-exist, six Jays and two Ells, in that hinterland of the 'least-worst' scenario. Another *This'll have to do*.

And after a while, it doesn't seem so bad.

On Hell, opinion is divided regarding this unsatisfactory state of affairs.

I TIRE OF the back tickle and check the time as I call a halt. Twenty-six minutes. Lily grunts, gets up, and goes to the sink. I follow her, and watch as she washes her face. Her boiler suit is still down to her waist, and I can see the top of her brand, burnt into her hip. Reflexively, I feel a twitch in my own brand, an ugly welt that is supposed to be a 4, but looks like a smudged triangle. I press a thumb to it and enjoy the bittersweet throb, like picking at a scab.

The brands are a relic of the era when the Overseers needed to be able to distinguish between brothers and sisters, in case there were any troublemakers. According to Mr Lee, in the early cycles they started with families of thirty or so identical brothers, unbranded, and the results were often anarchic. On one occasion, the Collection Ship arrived to find the Overseers lynched, the food stores destroyed, and the brothers all dead—some by starvation, some by their own hand.

They never made that mistake again. Social dynamics programming was developed, and different families of brothers and sisters were sent to the asteroids according to the algorithms. Branding was introduced, and the Overseers took tasers, not that there had ever been a need for them on Hell. Ours was a well-behaved little mining colony.

"What are you looking at?" Lily murmurs, as she finishes her ablutions.

"Your brand," I say. I look into the mirror over her shoulder and we stare at each other. I see my face reflected back at me all the time, but seeing two of my own face is unsettling and I look away. I suppose that's how the others feel all the time.

She turns around and pulls up her boiler suit. "You're a strange one, Leila."

"Well, if I'm strange, so are you."

"'Well, if I'm strange, so are you,'" she repeats back at me in a silly voice.

She's always bad-tempered in that period between waking and working—I would be just the same. We walk back in to the main cabin and collapse on our bunks at the same time.

A Jay—I think it's Jupiter, though it could be Joseph—wanders into our cabin without announcement, and picks up two long metal poles resting against one of the bunks. He nods at us and walks out.

"Would it kill them to knock?" Lily asks.

"We could do with a lock, like the Overseers," I say.

She picks at her lip. "Why exactly do they need locks anyway?"

"They have some private stuff, no?"

"What—in the cabinet by their cots?"

I nod. I have only ever been in Mr Lee's cabin, but I assume it is the same for Mr Reynolds and Mr Ortiz.

"But what private stuff?" she says. "What could they possibly own on Hell that could be secret or need locking up?"

I shrug. "Who knows—maybe they've been conditioned that way. Must be weird for them here, after Earth."

We sit in silence for a while, both contemplating what possible secret our kindly, fussy Mr Lee could be keeping. In the books I've read, characters often have a secret from their wives, or the police, or Victorian society. Here, however, the Overseers can do what they want—the Collection Ship is not coming for six hundred cycles, and until then, they're in charge. They don't *need* secrets.

I close my eyes and try to imagine a world where I'm carrying a dark secret that nobody else knows about, something nobody could have guessed about me; but I come up with a blank picture, and open my eyes.

THIRTY MINUTES LATER, and Lily is off on the way to her work shift. Technically I am due a sleep shift, but I feel restless and head out the cabin to try and shake it off. The tunnel connecting our cabin to the spine is maybe ten metres long, and lit by a single gloomy bulb. I turn left at the spine, past the tunnels to the Ays' and Bees' cabins, and down towards the communal areas. There are probably twelve people on base not on a work shift at the moment, and yet the silence is suffocating, apart from a dull buzz coming from some generator.

As I get closer to the communal areas, I hear voices and movement. I open the door and step into the Leisure cabin. Two Ays, Andy and Ashton, appear to be arm-wrestling, while Brenda is on a sofa, curled in a spiral. Brenda ignores me, while the Ays greet me and beckon me over to watch.

The two men are bare-chested, and their dark skin is glistening in the glare of the spotlight directly above them. Standing behind Andy, I can see a small pool of sweat gathering in the nape of his neck. Ashton has the edge of the contest, and, millimetre by millimetre, is pushing back Andy's straining arm—he hits the tipping point and the arm wrestle is suddenly over. He whoops and jumps up, while Andy collapses in his chair, covering his face with long, callused fingers.

I glance at Brenda and we smirk at each other in a moment of sisterhood—this sort of display would only be possible from an Ay. Their role in the mines is the graft, the tough labour at the rock face. They're built for it, and it seeps into their personality—strength means everything. Since they are genetically identical, they spend much of their free time working out how to get an edge over their brothers—running, lifting weights, boxing. In their cabin is an enormous, tedious chart of exactly how much ore has been cut by each brother, including Avery's, whose tally is stopped poignantly short. Of course, not all ore is equal, and some will yield far less metal or be unusable, but that subtlety escapes them. It is all about the brute force and machismo.

As if to prove the point, Ashton, grinning at Brenda, pounds his chest and roars, "Boom! Come *on!*"

THE AYS TRY to assert their individuality with the most superficial of methods:

Andrew has a shaved head.

Ashton wears a pair of glasses with no lenses, lent to him by one of the Overseers.

Alistair does this weird thing where he draws thick black lines on his cheeks with some pens he found, like war paint. But it fades and sometimes his face just looks a bit dirty for a while until he remembers to re-do them.

Nobody really knows what he's trying to achieve with this look.

Andy has grown a moustache (I love the fact that Mr Ortiz's imagination failed him so completely that when he named the Ays he had to use 'Andy' as well as 'Andrew').

Aaron is always wearing a baseball cap.

And Avery, right up to his untimely death, had enormous sideburns—they looked ridiculous, in my opinion.

They are not bad men, but I pity them. Despite their fig-leaf efforts, they remain incapable of the slightest independent thought. One cycle, to amuse myself, I prepared five questions and had a conversation with all of them separately. Their responses were almost identical, in some cases verbatim. My favourite:

Me: "Wow, you've been working hard, those muscles are bulging."

Andy/Andrew/Aaron/Ashton/Alistair: "Damn right they are. Careful you don't make (*insert relevant Bee here*) jealous now." Then they all winked.

ANDY HAS DISAPPEARED back to his cabin, and Ashton wanders off in the direction of the weights in the corner of Leisure. Brenda moves to make space on the sofa, and motions for me to take a seat. Although I'm never sure how much the Bees like us, they are always interesting company, so I sit down, and she curls around me, and starts to groom my hair. We sit like this in companionable silence for a few minutes.

"You should grow this out," she says. "You and Lily. You've got lovely hair, you should make the most of it."

"Hmm," I say.

Lily and I hate our hair, black and straight, and have both cropped it short and elfin. The Bees, on the other hand, have wavy chestnut tresses, and I have to stop myself from reaching out to stroke it. They have pale skin, wide blue eyes that draw you in, and dainty chins. Their faces are often serious, but when they laugh, it's with a throaty, infectious giggle.

It is rarely a problem telling them apart, but unlike the Ays, this is not down to superficial props. Different speech modulations, different mannerisms, different personality traits—I'm not even sure I could tell you *how* I know this one is Beatrice or that one is Bess; there's just a subconscious identification going on when you look at them. Did they do this deliberately, or was it organic? I'm not sure even *they* know.

Brenda is one of my favourite of the Bees—sometimes she pays me no attention, especially if an Ay is around— but if we're alone she is warm to me, and tells me gossip and makes me laugh.

We are facing the broad window surveying the galaxy of stars.

"Beautiful, isn't it?" I say.

"They all look alike, if you ask me."

"Do you know," I say, "Mr Reynolds pointed at one of them and said it was Earth."

"Reynolds," says Brenda with infinite disdain—I love that she calls him 'Reynolds' instead of 'Mr Reynolds'—

"knows as much about astronomy as I do about *pig farming*. Remember that next time he's droning on about it."

I giggle and she grins back at me.

"One of the things I've figured out is that the Overseers don't *actually* know that much. In fact," she says, dropping her voice to a mock-conspiratorial whisper, "they don't know a goddamn thing!"

She cackles loudly, and Ashton looks up from his corner, eyebrows raised.

"Not a goddamn thing," she repeats, and this time I can't stop myself from joining in with her cackle.

2

SWAG

I AM SHARING a jeep with Brenda, Bess, Juan and Jolly; one of the two Jays—not sure which—is driving. It is the yellow jeep, nicknamed Banana. We are on our way to East 3, a sector with a high concentration of tunnels and mineshafts, in the process of being bled dry of all its metals. The ground is uneven, and my head bounces and judders in time with the bumps. We are all in our suits, scratched and dirty, but lightweight and easy to move around in. Our heads are covered by a hood that connects to the suit, with a plastic visor for us to look out. We are squeezed together in the back, and I can feel Juan or Jolly next to me, his hip pressed against mine.

The Jays are small, but tough and wiry—though in their suits they just look small. I once read the phrase 'tough as old boots,' and I thought that fitted them perfectly—with their black leathery skin, and the sense they could bend and bend, but would never snap. If, for some reason, we had a civil war on Hell, I can't help feeling the Jays would be the last ones standing.

There's a crackle, and Juan or Jolly, whichever is next to me, speaks into my channel. We are inches apart but he doesn't even incline his head towards me as he speaks, which is just the kind of annoying but faintly amusing thing the Jays do all the time.

"*Leila. Hello. This is the first time in… twenty-eight cycles that we've shared a work shift,*" he says, his voice blurred by hissing and static. Bess, on his other side, glances at him: she can see he's speaking but unable to hear him.

"How do you know?" I reply.

"*The Rota archive,*" he says, in the clipped staccato the Jays always use. "*It was barely five minutes' work to find out.*"

"So what's your point?"

I hear the ghost of a smile through the static. "*No point. Just observing. I've seen your sister on several occasions recently, but not you.*"

"Who are you, anyway? Juan or Jolly?"

"*What makes you assume we're Juan and Jolly?*" cuts in the same voice, but with slightly different interference, and I'm annoyed to realise the second Jay has been listening on the channel.

"You're both down on the Rota for this shift," I say. "And shouldn't you be focussing on driving?"

"*Pfft,*" says a Jay, I've lost track which now. "*The Rota. What makes you think we follow the Rota?*"

"You have brands, no?"

"*The Overseers haven't checked our brands for a long time,*" says a Jay, and the other responds with a raspy laugh.

THE FUNDAMENTAL PROBLEM with the Jays is that they lack an Overseer to manage them. Overseer Fedorchuk came down to Hell with them, and named them—he died a long time ago. None of us can remember what he looked like or how he died, and the other Overseers won't talk about him. It must have been soon after our arrival for it to be so shrouded in mystery. But regardless, none of the three Overseers has yet taken responsibility for them. Mr Ortiz is in charge of the Ays, Mr Reynolds the Bees—really it should be Mr Lee, with his two sole charges, but he has so far managed to avoid that conversation.

As a result, provided the Jays do their job and don't cause too much disruption, they have license to run riot. The only way to distinguish them is with knowledge of the Rota, and the assumption they are following it. Sometimes I'm certain they are deliberately clouding their identities—just for the fun of it, I assume; I can never see much purpose—but short of ripping off their clothes and examining their brands, there's no way to prove anything.

The Jays' great passion is chess. One of the items sent down for Leisure was a single miniature chessboard, with plastic black and white pieces. A white rook is long lost and has been replaced with a drill bit. They run a simple system—whichever Jay is in possession of the board, keeps it until another Jay beats him. In the event of a stalemate, the holder keeps the board—and needless to say, between identical brothers, there are a lot of stalemates. So to wrest the board away from his brother, a Jay has to become more and more aggressive, take uncharacteristic risks. And the longer a Jay can hold on to the board, the more he can crow over his brothers.

Do they (could they) ever deceive each other? Swap identities mid-game? Would it make any difference? A few times, I have sat down to watch a game—two mirror images, hunched over the tiny board, both staring at it without the slightest movement. Once, it was Jupiter and Juan playing, I must have sat there for over twenty minutes while Jupiter decided on his move—the result was a pawn, moving forward one square. I could swear the two of them were deliberately slowing down their play, for their own amusement.

I CLEAR THE trailer of debris, and lug it over by its rope to the jeep. The two Jays have already disappeared into a mineshaft, where their heavy-duty machinery is found, and the Bees are listening to Mr Reynolds, who is pointing towards the top of a ridge. It's their role to do their tests and predict where the rich seams of metal are going to be found—to map out the whole asteroid while we do our best to take it apart.

A small mountain of jet-black ore—'swag,' as our little community likes to dub it—is waiting for me at the mineshaft entrance. I lean down and take a piece in my gloves, rubbing my fingers against the gritty texture. Then I pick up a shovel, and start to load the rocks into the trailer. Soon I am in a rhythm, a mindless repetition of digging and chucking, digging and chucking. There is no sound in the vacuum around me, but my imagination fills in the clatter the rocks ought to be making as they land in the trailer.

After some time, Andrew crawls out the mineshaft, dragging another load behind him on a tarpaulin. His suit is streaked with black. He must be exhausted, but he picks up a shovel and starts helping me to load up.

We are nearing the end of the pile of swag when he turns to me and speaks on my channel. "*You know, you need to have a word with your sister,*" he says.

"A word?"

"*Yeah. My brothers aren't happy. She keeps sticking her nose into our business.*"

"What business?" I say.

He shakes his giant hooded head. "*Questions, questions, too many damn questions. Just tell her to back off.*"

"I have no idea what you're talking about."

He lifts an enormous rock with his shovel, and hurls it into the trailer. "*Speak with her.*"

Then he stomps off and ducks his head back into the mineshaft.

SOME TIME LATER, I am at the ore depot, a giant circular vat packed with thousands of crates of metal ore. It is scarcely credible to think that a single one of those crates would make me a rich woman on Earth. In the same way, I suppose, there must be millions of chessboards on Earth, but if you were to destroy the Jays' single board, a new one would be ridiculously overvalued here.

The books on Mr Lee's reader are mainly from the nineteenth and twentieth centuries, so I can't glean much information there about what happened to the metals, but from what Mr Lee tells me, they started to run out in the twenty-first century. Lead was the first to go, followed in quick succession by zinc, platinum and nickel. Dozens of rare metals too, all crucial to the production of everyday items like cars, phones and televisions. All original elements, impossible to synthetically reproduce.

It had been known for years that huge quantities of these metals were to be found on M-Type asteroids like Mizushima-00109, but nothing was done until the reserves ran out. Even then, they had to come up with a solution of who to send out to the asteroids. Unless they were paid exorbitant wages like the Overseers, nobody else was crazy enough to come out here for a stretch of seven Earth years.

Until us. We, of course, are working for our passage to Earth. And in a masterstroke of efficiency, we're also mining our own fuel—courtesy of the hydrated minerals we dig up, to be broken down into hydrogen and oxygen.

The Jays sometimes make bitter comments about the fact we even have to fuel our own trip to Earth, but really, it seems churlish to complain about our status. We were brought into existence for this express purpose. The scientists back on Earth, who made us possible, are God-like figures—it's not for us to question their decisions and quibble about logistics. I've put my trust in them, and our future on Earth.

I CAN VAGUELY recall a time when Mr Ortiz gave us a speech about the importance of what we were doing here. Spirits were low for some reason or another, our quotas were down, and Mr Ortiz has always fancied himself as something of a motivator. We were all gathered in the Community cabin, it must have been the General Asteroid Meeting that takes place every hundred cycles.

"This simple black rock," he said—for he had brought a prop with him, a chunk of swag the size of his fist— "will be worth several thousand dollars back on Earth. Do you all realise the value of what we're doing here?"

Twenty blank faces stared back at him.

"Every two hundred cycles—*two hundred cycles*—our small team mines more nickel than would have been mined on Earth over a twenty-year period. We're pioneers! You're going to be heroes when you get back to Earth!"

I paraphrase, of course. I can only loosely remember what he said, and I've made him more eloquent than he really is. All my memories seem to blur, until they're no more than a series of frozen images, woven together by my imagination.

INSIDE THE DEPOT, under the solar-powered lanterns, my real work begins. The swag needs to be sorted into crates depending on what they contain. Water rocks are the easiest—you can spot the stress fractures on the outside where the frozen water has expanded. The different metals are harder—first I pass a supermagnet over them to check they contain some metals. Occasionally there is nothing—the Bees sometimes get it wrong when making their calculations—but generally even the smallest traces are worth keeping.

Then I proceed with a series of tests to separate out the different metals—dabbing with a solution of hydrochloric acid to check for nickel ore (the surface turns red), or another pungent acid that remains colourless when applied to platinum ore. It is long, repetitive work—often unrewarding, since after eight hours of sorting, the depot will look scarcely any different from when I started: some ore from crate A now in crate B, some ore from crate B now in crate A, *ad infinitum*.

I don't kid myself about the work I do—I don't need the physical strength of the Ays, the intelligence of the Bees, or the technical skill of the Jays. If it had been cheaper to send robots to do our work, robots would doubtless have been employed. But it would be absurd to be embarrassed by the role we play, considering it's a role for which we were bred. And it takes a certain discipline too, to categorise all these rocks, without ever losing track. Mr Lee likes to call us archivists, and sometimes privately pooh-poohs the works done by the others. "Blessed be the archivists!" he will say, and I don't really know what he means but I laugh anyway.

I TAKE A break to hydrate myself through a straw—as always, I leave the depot to sit on the rubble outside, and stare into the black infinity ahead of me. It is cold out on the surface, even with the foam insulation that lines our suits, and I have to keep myself moving to stay warm, shaking my hands, waggling my toes. The East 3 dig site is only a five-minute drive away, but I can see nothing ahead of me except the black, empty desert. It occurs to me that living in these conditions could send a person mad, if they had spent their previous life on Earth as the Overseers have. To go from rivers, rainforests, beaches, cities, farms—all concepts I can only attempt to visualise—to this silent, barren land; it must feel like a prison to them.

Conversely, even though I feel like I ought to dislike its emptiness, its silence, I cannot. Earthbound humans may crave the colour and noise of their homeland, but I daresay if they had been born here in Hell, they would have learnt to value its un-Earthness.

I wonder to myself, is this is how it feels to be in a mother's womb? Sealed off from the outside—no noise, no colour, no movement. But then, who knows what it's like to be in the womb, maybe it's an explosion of sensations? This is exactly the kind of line of questioning that gets me funny looks from the Overseers.

My problem is that I read too much. Mr Lee's reader— it's been a blessing and a curse. All the time, I'm soaking up these images of a foreign world, one that couldn't be more different to our own. But try and apply to Hell what you learn about Earth, and you get in all sorts of trouble.

"A little knowledge is a dangerous thing," Mr Lee once said, sounding very wise, but then he's the bugger that lent me the reader.

AFTER EIGHT HOURS of repetitive tedium, it's time to move on. Next to the ore depot is the stores depot where we keep our supplies. I drive Banana and the trailer over there. Water, dried food, medical supplies and oxygen tanks are found here, as well as all our construction tools. It is surrounded by a vast shell: the body of the shuttle that first brought us and our supplies down from the master ship. The quantities seem staggering—at the rate we're going, it will last another three orbits, plenty to last the next set of brothers and sisters who come here to replace us in six hundred cycles. I wonder if they'll stick with the same combination of Ays, Bees, Jays and Ells.

That would be bizarre, if six new Ells turned up. Like going back in time, to see myself when I first arrived. I doubt they'd want us to see each other, though. Cross-contamination or something, like platinum and nickel ore in the same crate. Except that's not really the same, is it? Not everything can be compared with asteroid mining.

I load up the trailer with supplies, as requested by Mr Reynolds—food and water, and a bundle of wires, needed by the Jays to help fix one of the heavy-duty drills. I get into Banana, and off I go back to East 3. It's dark now, even more so than when Juan (or Jolly) was driving us earlier, and I can barely make out any details of the landscape, just the solar-powered lantern by the mineshaft. The jeep pitches and staggers about as I drive blindly on, trusting to instinct to keep it upright, and this seems to work. Nobody is waiting when I arrive, so I pull up by the mineshaft and turn off the power.

I step out and peer into the mineshaft. Lanterns are strung out at regular intervals, like fairy lights. I have been down the shafts a few times, when all available hands were required to help repair a tunnel boring machine or clear a collapse. Usually you can stoop your head and walk, crab-like, at the start of the tunnel. The Jays reinforce the sides with concrete and steel, and it feels pretty safe, like an extension of the base. But further down, you have to get on your hands and knees to crawl, and the tunnels become more ragged—dust everywhere, and brittle, crumbling swag on the floor. The Ays, who spend hours down the shafts, pick up dozens of scrapes and bruises (which of course they are not shy of sharing with everyone else, if only as an excuse to take their tops off).

They are horrible places.

Lily has a morbid fear of getting stuck down one, and avoids them at all possible cost. Just a few cycles ago, I remember we were both on shift at the same time—me in the ore depot, she in the stores—and she tapped into my suit channel.

"*Lei, did you see Aaron? He had a big red gash down his thigh. A strut collapsed—a big chunk of swag fell down and trapped his leg.*"

"Like Avery," I said.

"*Yeah. But the thing about Aaron—it was the end of his shift, Andy came to find him. Imagine if that had happened at the start of your shift, and you were stuck down there for hours and hours. You can't move in any direction, your face shoved up against the wall…*" There was an audible shudder.

"You'd just have to blank out," I said. "Retreat somewhere else in your mind."

"*Are you crazy? Just forget about it, ho-hum, let's go to a pretty place in my head?*"

"It's not so different from when we're back in the cabin," I pointed out. "You've got a bit more space to move your body, but not that much. I'd far rather spend the time in my head."

Lily made no reply, but I could hear her breathing, and I knew she was considering it; then the breathing stopped and I knew she was thinking about being trapped in a tunnel again.

3

AN UNFORTUNATE ACCIDENT

THE ROTA TAKES pride of place in the Community cabin—a grid of three by six giant sheets of paper, showing the consecutive cycles, and what everyone is doing every hour of every cycle. Every five cycles, the leftmost pieces of paper are removed for archiving, and everything is shifted to the left. Only the Overseers can add to or amend the Rota (well, they're the only ones who have learned to write). Notionally, all three Overseers are responsible, but it is Mr Ortiz's labour of love, evident in every perfect line and immaculately shaded square.

It is the single most boring thing ever created on Hell.

I mean, I don't object to a rota in principle, and I daresay Mr Ortiz's scheduling is the most efficient way to go about our work, but there's something about it that makes me want to vomit. The Ays treat it as their sacred text, and even the Bees have a tendency to be less cynical than usual when confronted with it.

Mr Ortiz often overcomplicates the Rota, searching for the algorithms that will optimise our performance and keep up with our quotas. I have walked into the Community cabin before, to find him standing, hands on hips, surveying the Rota, eyebrows knitted in furious concentration. Personally, I think he has too much time on his hands. Unlike the Bees (or even we two Ells), the Ays don't need a lot of guidance—there's not a lot he can tell them. He strikes me as the most directionless person on the asteroid, desperately looking for a purpose here, a way to contribute.

I HAVE WOKEN up from a sleep shift, and am standing by the Rota, figuring out when I will see Lil. She is due back in the next hour, leaving a window of two hours before my next work shift. I turn my back on the Rota, and decide to pay a visit to Mr Lee. Up the spine I go, past our tunnel, past the Ays' and Bees' tunnels—muffled, angry voices—to the end of the spine, which bifurcates twice into the tunnels for Messrs Ortiz, Reynolds and Lee—and Mr Fedorchuk's old cabin.

I take the far left tunnel, and knock three times briskly on the door of Mr Lee's cabin.

"Enter," he says, and in I go.

"Hello, Leila," he says.

"Hello."

His face is pale, and he is sat on his cot, palms on his knees.

"Everything okay?" I ask.

"Marvellous," he says. "What news?"

"Just wanted to check in. I need a recommendation."

One of the quirks of our relationship is that our interaction is largely via the medium of a sort of book club, discussing the literature of a culture (nineteenth, twentieth century Britain and America) that is barely relevant to contemporary Earth, let alone contemporary Hell.

Before leaving Earth, Mr Lee managed to fill his reader with hundreds of old English language texts, from Hardy to Roth. At some point, after I'd been pestering him with questions about Earth, he lent the reader to me, and I greedily gobbled up *The Go-Between*, about a world he admitted bore no resemblance to the one he had left. But a beautiful world, all the same. From there, I never looked back. He let me borrow it again and again, working my way through Waugh, Austen, Orwell, Updike, and countless others I've forgotten.

At the moment, I am going through an Agatha Christie phase. "I've finished *Endless Night*," I say. "Need something new."

"What did you think?"

"Loved it. The Poirots and Marples can be a bit neat, you know? A bit too pat."

"Like crossword puzzles."

"Right. But when she ditches the detectives, you really

start to feel for the characters. I mean, with a Poirot murderer, they're just a puzzle you've got to solve, you don't really see them as people. But here, it's sad, because you don't want the murderer to be evil, and you realise it's been staring at you in the face the whole time."

"You should try Dorothy Sayers," he says, "or even Ngaio Marsh. They're from the same era, I think you'd like them."

"How come there's so many of these murder mystery books?" I ask. "Were there loads of murders back then?"

"I don't think so. Most people live pretty humdrum lives, you know. And a murder is a pretty horrific thing to happen."

He stands up abruptly. He always looks uneasy in his body, like it's the wrong size for him or something. Mr Ortiz and Mr Reynolds look completely at home in their boiler suits and plain tunics, but with Mr Lee—dainty, even smaller than the Jays—you feel like he belongs in something tailored, in the bold colours you can see on the posters the Overseers brought with them.

I wonder if he's on the pills that the Overseers have—supposedly they're just to help them sleep, though we all think they're more than that; whenever Mr Reynolds has too many, he acts bizarrely, talking gibberish, and one of the Bees has to take him back to his cabin. Mr Lee and Mr Ortiz don't seem to take them so much, but even they occasionally seem a bit out of it.

Mr Lee wanders over to his filing cabinet, where a small photograph stands, of his wife and two children. He doesn't talk about them much.

He scratches at a point below his ear, a tic he does all the time. "I wish I'd brought a p-book with me," he says. "They take a while to get used to, but you'd have liked them."

My reply is cut off as there is a knock at the door, and Mr Reynolds walks in, without waiting for a reply.

"Wotcher," he says. "Not interrupting anything, am I?" Even at the best of times, his voice is an ugly leer. When I hear it, my muscles tense and I find myself squeezing my fingers together.

They try not to show it in front of us, but Mr Lee and Mr Reynolds heartily dislike each other. Mr Lee betrays himself with blank politeness, Mr Reynolds by the way he swaggers around him, like an animal squaring up for a fight. Mr Lee never says anything, but I can tell. Their faces both say they're spoiling to thrash out an argument one of these cycles, but I guess when there are just three of you, you can't afford to make enemies.

"What can I do for you?" Mr Lee says, turning his back and busying himself with nothing.

Mr Reynolds steps closer to him, ignoring me. His scraggy beard bristles, like it's alive. He is the biggest person on Hell, but his movements are slow and ponderous—I'd fancy an Ay or a Jay in a fight with him.

"One of your girls," Mr Reynolds says, with a sideways glance at me, "never turned up for her shift."

Mr Lee turns. "What?"

"L3," he says, "she went AWOL—one of my girls was driving a shift over to East 9, they waited half an hour for her—she never showed."

"Who from your team?"

"B4 and B6. They just got back." He doesn't always talk like this, sometimes he uses our names, but other times it's like he's trying to make some kind of point—whatever it is, it's too subtle for me to work out, or care.

Mr Lee looks over at me. "You know anything about this?"

I shrug. "I haven't seen *Lily*"—I resist the impulse to meet Mr Reynolds' eyes—"for two cycles. Must be some cock-up with the Rota."

Mr Reynolds stares at me hard, then juts his chin in my direction. "Check her brand," he says. "Make sure there's no funny games going on."

My brand twitches. "That'll do," Mr Lee snaps. "This is Leila, I know my girls. Now, why don't we go to the Rota, and see what we can see?"

The three of us head out of Mr Lee's cabin, into the spine, Mr Reynolds marching ahead.

"Bess," he barks, and I hear movement in the Bees' cabin, and then unhurried footsteps, as Bess comes to follow us.

Into the Community cabin, which is empty—though there are a few noises coming from the Leisure cabin, a few feet away from us. The four of us approach the Rota, and Mr Reynolds slaps a meaty finger on the relevant square, showing Lily on the shift, along with two Bees and two Ays. The Bees have since returned in Tomato (the red buggy), leaving the Ays working down the mineshafts.

Mr Lee frowns. "She can't have gone with the previous shift. The Jays have taken Banana and Cabbage out to the south."

Four of the Jays, with two Bees and Mr Ortiz, were scouting out a new site in South 4, and exploring how easy it was to dig there. There was no way Lily could have joined them by mistake—or that the others would have even let her.

"In which case," says Mr Reynolds, "she must be on the base somewhere."

"Did you try suit comms?" Mr Lee asks Bess sharply.

"Of course," she says. "Nothing."

"Let's start looking, then," says Mr Reynolds.

"Leila and I will take care of it," Mr Lee says.

"Not at all," says Mr Reynolds, grinning widely. "The more, the merrier."

We search in silence. 'Search' is perhaps over-egging it—we peer around the door of each cabin; there's nowhere to hide in them, not really. In the Leisure cabin, Ashton is bench-pressing, while two of the Bees are talking. Our cabin is empty, the Jays' cabin has two sleeping Jays (Jupiter and Jolly, supposedly). Likewise, Andy and Alistair are asleep in theirs, and in the Bees' cabin, Betty is washing her face, suit half-removed after her shift.

Bess stays with her sister, and I walk up the spine with the two Overseers. We check the empty cabin of Mr Fedorchuk, and Mr Lee raps on the locked door of Mr Ortiz ("Just in case," he says), but there is no reply and we face each other.

"What now?" says Mr Reynolds, and the weird mixture of Mr Lee's irritation and Mr Reynolds' glee is gone now. Both men look wary. Needles of pain flare up at the base of my skull, like they always do in moments of stress.

"Let's count the suits," says Mr Lee, and off we go to the airlock where the suits are found, next to Mr Reynolds' cabin. He types in the code, the doors open, and we step into the airlock—just one set of doors now separating us from Hell's near-vacuum.

There were originally thirty-five suits, for the team of twenty-eight, with seven spares. Three suits are no longer functioning, so we have thirty-two left, of which ten should be in use at the moment. We count and double-count, but there are only twenty-one suits in the airlock.

"Okay," says Mr Lee. "So, she's out there somewhere. Leila, suit up, we'd better find her and make sure everything is alright."

"Well, hang on," says Mr Reynolds, "are you taking Tomato? Won't this mess up the Rota?"

"Bugger the Rota," says Mr Lee. "Go and inform the next shift of the changes."

Mr Reynolds retreats, with a glare at Mr Lee's back, and the two of us change into our suits. I type in the code for the outer doors, and we head towards Tomato. Beyond the glare of the base lights, it's dawn on Hell, another cycle fast beginning. As always, there's that numb, ghostly sensation as you step outside, like breaching the skin of a giant bubble, and it sealing up again behind you. By an unspoken agreement, I climb into Tomato's driving seat, and Mr Lee gets in next to me. He hates driving; he'll do it if he has to, but with none of the relish that the other two Overseers display when controlling the jeeps.

"*Let's check out the depots first,*" Mr Lee says to me on my channel. "*It's got to be the most likely place.*"

"Sure thing."

Metal poles have been forced into the ground, pointing in different directions, acting as rough signposts. I do a U-turn, and set a course for the depots. Neither of us seems to be in the mood for conversation. I focus on driving Tomato, which for some reason feels more difficult in the sunlight, when you can see every bump and crack on the asteroid's surface. I drive fast, and can see Mr Lee's hand is gripping the door handle as we career down the slope to the depots.

We arrive at the ore depot, and I clamber out of the jeep. There is no sign of life, but then there never is. Just having two of us walk into the depot feels crowded, quite frankly. This is my realm, mine and Lily's, and on the rare occasions I have a visitor, I can barely stay still, so nervous I am about them moving some of the swag or knocking over the painstakingly arranged crates. Not that I'd ever say anything—I'm not that pathetic—but it's an instinct I can't fight. We don't have much of our own, Lily and I, but we have this, the depot, and you mess with it at your peril.

"Lily?" I call out loud, then realise I'm being stupid, then realise Mr Lee can't hear me either so I can say whatever I damn well like. I try her channel, again, but the only noise is the dead hum of a closed channel. Mr Lee makes some hand gestures that aren't very clear, I ignore them and we just spread out and walk up and down the rows of crates. Pretty soon, I know she's not here; it's a sense you get for these things when it's your sister.

The silence sounds the same as you always get on Hell, but it's different somehow too, heavier, more stifling. I pass crate after crate, idly brushing my fingers against the black chips that poke over the edges. This is a waste of time, I know it. I see Mr Lee peering around the edge of a crate, as though she's hiding there, legs tucked in, curled into herself like an embryo.

I connect to his channel. "She's not here," I say. "Stores next."

He turns, sees me, and nods without speaking. We climb into Tomato, and take the short hop to the stores.

As soon as we walk in, I see something's wrong. Boxes have been opened, the contents spilled across the floor. On the rows of shelves, water drums and gas canisters are no longer in neat lines but roughly shoved apart, creating fissures all along the rows.

"Someone's been here," I say to Mr Lee, and he raises his eyebrows.

"*Could it be Lily?*" he asks.

"Not impossible… but this mess—it's like they were trying to find something. Lily would have known exactly where everything was."

"*Okay. Who, then?*"

I shrug and take a look at the open boxes. Pouches of freeze-dried food lie scattered. Further into the stores, order seems to have returned, as though the intruder was hunting around and realised the impossible size of the task, so stormed out in frustration. The silence stretches out. And still no sign of Lily.

WHEN WE ARRIVE at the site of South 4, two figures are standing, unmoving, by Banana, as our jeep pulls up with a flurry of ore dust. One of them has a grey stripe running down his boiler suit—it must be Mr Ortiz—and Mr Lee opens a three-way channel with me.

"*We're looking for Lily,*" he says. "*Have you seen her?*"

"*Lily?*" says Mr Ortiz. "*No, why? What would she be doing here?*"

"*You didn't see her around when you left base?*"

"*Nope.*" A slight pause. "*Check the Rota, pal. How many times have I said it? The Rota is the final authority.*"

Mr Ortiz has been in a foul mood for the last few cycles, ever since his taser went missing. He threw some threats around, mainly at the Jays—but the general consensus is that he mislaid it somewhere out in the tunnels. There's a spare for him, but he's clearly not happy at being made to look a fool.

Mr Lee doesn't bother to respond. He drums his fingers on the dashboard, I can't hear it, but I feel the rhythm, *da-da-da da, da-da-da da*. "*Okay,*" he says. "*Where next?*"

"I don't understand," I say. "She can't have just walked off by herself. What's she playing at?"

There's a crackle as another channel is patched in, and the figure next to Mr Ortiz glances up at him. "*Jolly, they're looking for Lily,*" Mr Ortiz says. "*Any ideas?*"

All I can hear is the shallow breathing of the three men. "*Lily… Lily…*" Jolly muses. "*Let me think. I've seen her before in the tunnels. Talking to the Ays. Maybe she's there?*"

"Doesn't sound much like Lily," I say. "She hated the tunnels. Which ones?"

"*The warren in East 5,*" he says.

I glance at Mr Lee. It's where the two Ays are to be found, still working and waiting for relief. "I guess we should check it out," I say. "We're running out of other options."

Jolly offers to come with us, and the three of us set off for East 5, along a craggy path that climbs through the black dunes. It is silent in the jeep. I keep my eyes on the path and try to ignore the rising panic in my gut.

THERE IS NO sign of the Ays at East 5, nor even a hint as to which tunnel they're working in. I try their channels, but there is no signal. I try Lily's channel again, reflexively, hopelessly. Mr Lee seems to sense my nerves, and places his gloves on the small of my back. There's a crackle as he patches through a three-way, and then he says: "*If you find Aaron or Andrew, bring them back and ask for their help.*"

Jolly says nothing. Jays are always good at knowing when to shoot their mouth off and when to shut up.

I pick a tunnel at random: the far-left mineshaft, hacked deep into the heart of Mizushima-00109. Somehow the silence is more eerie in the tunnels than outside. Soon I'm crouching, then I have to lie down on the trolley and pull myself along. The trolley rattles along the ruts, and my bones rattle too. How do the Ays put up with this, cycle after cycle?

After a few minutes pulling, I can see the end of the shaft, with temporary struts holding up the roof. I turn around, squeezing up against the walls, and a haze of dust and swag crumbs rains down on me. I pull myself back the way I've come; there's already a dull ache in my arms, and everything seems to be happening in slow motion. I choose another branch, and on I go.

On the fourth and final branch of the tunnel set, I spot that the trolley is missing. I hunker down on my knees, and shuffle forwards. I try the Ays' channels, and this time there is a signal. Andrew answers back, suspicious: "*Leila?*"

"Andrew! Have you seen Lily?"

"*What, down here? You serious?*"

"We can't find her anywhere, Andrew. I'm getting worried."

"*Hold on.*"

After a minute's wait, I make out Andrew on the trolley, paddling forwards, quicker and more fluid than I could ever manage. He reaches me and the two of us leave the mineshaft together, Andrew having to crouch nearly until the end. He asks me questions, but I can tell he's impatient, confident there's a simple explanation, that the Rota is being mucked about for no reason (not to mention his quota). He makes a cursory examination of the other shafts, as though I might have brushed past her by accident—and we go out onto the open plains of Hell.

And then I see her.

Forty feet away, by a dune that allows access to several tunnels, Jolly is next to her prostrate body, standing helplessly. He's holding her hood, and I can see my sister's face turned towards me. Her lips are blue, and her eyes are bulging slightly. There is something obscene about the sight, human flesh exposed on the surface of Hell for the first time.

Lily. My sister. My last sister.

And as I make my way towards them, with giant leaps, all I can think of is that now I'm just a one, Leila all alone, and it's as though a part of me has just died.

4

MARPLE

I LIE ON my cot, legs akimbo, and ponder the question, 'What would Miss Marple do?' She would not go trampling in, interrogating suspects and getting everyone's back up. No, the Marple technique is to casually engage suspects in conversation, and in a meandering way, get them to reveal facts they didn't intend to. And she would come up with some insights into human psychology, based on her knowledge of village life—a butcher who overcharged his customers, a vicar who fell out with his rector, etcetera.

I can't exactly fall back on that skill, but I can still take the subtle Marple approach to my investigation into Lily's murder.

And contrary to the mutterings I heard back at the base, it *was* murder, not a terrible accident (or suicide, an even more preposterous suggestion). I saw the bruises on her neck, the small tears in the material where Lily and her killer struggled for control of the hood's clasp.

And then? Did the killer turn away or stand and watch? It'd take a cold, cold bastard to watch while she ran out of oxygen and choked to death, scrabbling around in the dust of Hell. Jolly found her at the end of a tunnel, and the back of her suit was coated in black dust, suggesting the killer dragged her inside the warren of tunnels, before pushing her to the end on a trolley. It would have been a risk—they could have easily been seen—but it seems the gamble paid off.

The journey back to the base has a strange, dream-like quality to it. It's a squash, I remember, because we bring back the two Ays as well as Lily's body. But I can't picture who's driving, or what anyone says, all I remember is sitting at one side, with my sister's head lolling in my lap, and Mr Lee next to me, squeezing my glove in his. Lily's startled expression, a reflection on my own. And I can't look away, can't drag my eyes away from my sister's. I won't let go of her when we get back to the base. Gentle gloves support me as I carry her back to our cabin.

They buried Avery deep in the ore, submerged in the swag that he spent his life excavating. I don't think that's what Lily would want, but what else can we do with her?

One thing: at least I don't have to worry about

forgetting Lily's face or voice, like I did with Overseer Fedorchuk. I can look in a mirror whenever I want— even pretend I'm having a conversation with her.

"Would that be weird, Lil?" I glance up at her body— top bunk, under a sheet, face decorously turned to face a wall.

"You're right, it would be weird."

I think back to our last conversation—Lily sleepy and cranky; I obsess for some time about her exact last words to me, trying to imbue them with some significance. Then I give up and conclude it was something humdrum. I do remember her talking about our four sisters though, and how we have to look out for each other, and I know I have to do this, have to do a Marple.

There will be objections, of course there will. For most of the citizens of Hell, the slightest change in their precious routines causes existential panic. But they can't stop me. What exactly would they do to me? Particularly since, as the last remaining Ell on the asteroid, I hold a small degree of bargaining power.

The first thing to ascertain is whether Lily has left behind any sign of what she was up to, that might have triggered her murder. I bound up from my cot like a spring and start to hunt, digging my fingers under the spare mattress. I poke around every corner and gap, hoping to find something abnormal. I climb the ladder to where her body is, and with an embarrassed laugh-slash-gulp start to delve in her suit pockets. My finger brushes against the sole of her foot, and it is as cold and hard as a piece of swag. It doesn't take long to do a proper search of the cabin, and it is when I'm on my knees, peering underneath the cot, that I see the marks.

I pull the cot away from the wall—a terrible, shrill squeal of metal. I sit cross-legged on the cot and stare down at the scratches that have been gouged out of the floor. Next to them is the offending instrument, a chunk of swag that is glistening but dull and razed down at one end. The marks look like this:

$$\cancel{||||}$$
$$||$$
$$||$$
$$\cancel{||||}\ |$$

I blink at them several times, trying to fix them in my brain, then push the cot back in case anyone comes in. Lily must have done this, alone in our cabin, arm stretched down behind the cot, working hurriedly in case anyone disturbed her.

"Okay," I say out loud. "Interesting. I didn't know you had secrets from me, Lil."

I imagine I'm Lily, lying on my cot, ankles crossed the way we both do, bringing out that piece of swag she'd smuggled in. This had been planned, it wasn't some sudden, vandalistic scrawl. What was she trying to create? A message? A reminder? A tally?

I am considering this for some time, when Ashton enters and surveys me cautiously. "Are you coming with us on shift?" he says.

He's not wearing his glasses. Ashton always wears his glasses. "Where are your glasses?" I say.

"I don't know," he says. "I woke up one cycle and they were gone. Are you coming with us on shift?"

"You'll have to get started without me," I say. "I need to… thrash out a few things first."

He seems about to say something, but stops himself.

"Okay," he says and leaves the cabin. I decide it's time to pay Mr Ortiz a visit.

MR ORTIZ IS a man who weighs out every movement and gesture carefully. He stands on the threshold of his cabin, not inviting me in, listening to me without interrupting or shifting around impatiently like Mr Reynolds would do. He has the same brown skin as the Ays, but in the glare of the light, I notice how rough he looks—face covered in stubble and dust, a rash of pockmarks on his cheeks.

"So let me get this straight," he says. "You want me to investigate if Lily was killed?"

"It's more *by whom*, not *if*," I say. "There can't really be any doubt it was murder. And I'm happy to be the one who investigates it. She was my sister, after all."

He smiles tightly. It's like he's deciding whether to shout at me or put a comforting arm round my shoulder. Mr Ortiz's great problem is that he can't decide whether he wants to be liked, respected or feared.

"Here's the problem, Leila," he says. "Putting aside the question of how and when you'd do this 'investigation'—"

"I'd do it during my Leisure shifts," I say.

"Putting that aside," he presses on, "what authority are you operating under exactly? By which I mean, let's say you ask all your 'questions,' and at the end announce that it was—"

He breaks off and looks theatrically up at the ceiling.

"Jolly," he says. "It was Jolly who must have killed her, you're sure of it."

"So…"

"But Jolly says it *wasn't* him, and his word counts just as much as your conjectures."

"But—"

"What I'm trying to say, darling, is we have no police force here. No forensic analyst, no murder squad. We're a self-policing community—which means we, the Overseers, enforce discipline and keep the peace."

"I'll find proof," I say. "I'll find who did it, and bring you proof."

"And then what?" he says, spreading his arms wide. "We hold a trial? Who's going to be the judge—you? What, we're going to have a little jury of Ays and Bees and Jays?"

"Look," I say. "Just listen."

He peers round. "And where's the prison? Because we're a bit cramped in here, in case you hadn't noticed. Are you going to shut the murderer up in your cabin, and be the jailer as well?"

I clench my teeth to stop myself speaking. Mr Ortiz is an intelligent man, a different type of intelligence to Mr Lee—but he can also be a poisonous twat sometimes.

"I'm going to do this," I say. "I wasn't asking for *permission*."

He sighs. "Look, when the Collection Ship comes, there'll be some other Ells, I guarantee you. Is that not…?"

"What, we're all the same, so what does it matter?"

"Ah, get off your high horse, I was just trying to help. Do what you want—I honestly don't care."

"I will."

"But if you start disrupting the work here, or irritating any of my boys, you'll have to answer for it."

He moves to close the door, but I say, "Hang on—I've got some questions for you."

He smirks. "What am I, a suspect?"

I ignore this. This never happened to Miss Marple—her technique is more difficult than I thought, mainly because I don't know how to engage Mr Ortiz in casual, meandering conversation.

"Will you please just do this for me?" I say. "I'm trying to figure out Lily's last movements. When did you see her last?"

He looks away sourly. "I don't know. A few cycles ago? I haven't seen either of you lately, I've been busy on the new South site. You need to check with whoever was last on shift with her."

"Andrew spoke to me recently, he told me to tell Lily to back off, stop sticking her nose into the Ays' business. What's *that* about?"

"How should I know? I'm not their nanny. Ask one of them."

"Right," I say, deflated.

"Are we finished?"

"Who do you think could have killed her?"

"Assuming she *was* killed, which nobody's proved... you really want my opinion? In my experience, when people get killed, it's usually something to do with sex. So, your best bet has to be one of the Jays."

"But she wasn't with *any* of the Jays," I say.

"You sure about that?" he says, eyebrows raised.

A half-memory flits out my grasp, a fuzzy picture of a single bare leg and a burst packet of powdered milk. For a second I can smell the malty tang of the powder. There's something more there, something else that I wish I could remember... and it's gone. I realise I've closed my eyes—and when I open them, the door is shut and Mr Ortiz has vanished.

HOURS PASS. A check of the Rota reveals that I'm on shift again soon, taking Tomato out to East 3 with Mr Reynolds and a couple of Bees. Part of me considers not going, cracking on instead with my detective work. But quizzing Mr Reynolds will be easier out on the asteroid. Inside, the Overseers are in pressurised, oxygenated cabins, in control, and they know it. Bearding Mr Ortiz (and there's a good verb, *to beard*—you don't hear anyone use that out here) on the threshold of his cabin was a bad idea. But outside, the power dynamic is rather different. We're more comfortable there than the Overseers—we *belong*.

After a short spell of daydreaming in my cabin, still in the company of my sister's corpse, I make my way to the porch to suit up. Bess and Becci are already there, putting on their suits with elegant efficiency. They don't say anything to me, but Bess leans over and squeezes my hand, which I like. I realise it's the first skin-on-skin contact I've had for cycles and cycles. Who's going to tickle my back and stroke my feet now Lily's gone? And whose back am *I* going to tickle, whose feet will I stroke? Dark, dark times.

I pick a suit, patch in my channel, and start to get ready. I take the hood in my hands and stare at it in grim fascination. One heck of a murder weapon, a hood— or to be precise, hood removal. It feels like a rushed, spontaneous murder, but with a bit of planning, this could have been one of those perfect crimes. I get side-tracked thinking how I would commit a murder, but I can't think of anyone I'd want to kill and I give up.

The hood locks on with a barely perceptible *click*. Mr Reynolds stalks in, glances at me, nods. He looks morose, with dark rings under his dull blue eyes. He's lost the cockiness on display just a cycle ago, when we were right here with Mr Lee, hunting for Lily.

"You okay?" he says, not looking at me directly, awkward as a boy.

I nod, and soon we are ready—we load up Tomato, and we head out to East 3, Mr Reynolds at the wheel.

When we arrive, Aaron and two Jays are already on site, dragging a large drill towards one of the tunnel entrances. The Bees start climbing a dune, and Mr

Reynolds moves to follow them, but I patch into his channel: "Mr Reynolds? Can I ask you something?"

He stops and turns. "*Sure. Shoot.*"

I mentally pat myself on the back. Bearding him outside was an inspired decision. On base, in the flesh, he can't help but be reminded of the us-and-them scenario. What does he see when he looks at me? A pesky, barely-human human—an L4. But on the surface of Hell, in our anonymous suits, we're both just animals trying to stay alive in the toxic atmosphere.

"I want to know who you think killed my sister," I say. There's no need to go blazing in, interrogating Mr Reynolds. For all his bluster, I know there's a sentimental soul there, far more so than Mr Ortiz, and I know he's dying to play the big hero. All *I* have to do is play the helpless little girl.

After a slight pause, the channel crackles with his gruff breathing, and he says, "*I don't know. Maybe we'll never know. Don't you think it'd be best to forget about it? Move on?*"

"But I really need to know, Mr Reynolds," I say. "Can't you help me?"

A sigh. "*Look, I'll have a word with the other Overseers. I'll see what we can do.*"

"I'm just worried, if they killed Lily, they might want to kill me too. And what if they go after one of your Bees?"

He scoffs. "*Yeah, well, let's be honest, if it was anyone, it's going to be one of the Ays or the Jays. But don't you worry. I can handle them.*"

"They might be working together, though. Two or three Ays, or even all five. They're going to stick up for each other, aren't they?"

Mr Reynolds turned towards the tunnels where the Ays were working. "*We'll see,*" he said. "*We've got a good thing going here, everyone's happy. If the Ays or Jays want to bring a war to Hell, we'll be ready for them.*"

"Listen," I said, changing track, "how do the Ays work it with the Bees, with just five of them and six Bees? Who goes with who?"

"*Why do you ask?*"

"Lily, she was asking the Ays a load of questions before she got killed. I'm just wondering if it had to do with that."

"*It was Barbara who was with Avery,*" he says. "*But they've all swapped partners a dozen times since then, it's like bloody musical chairs.*" I can hear the smirk in his voice.

"Seriously?"

"*Oh, yes. And it's the Bees who pull all the strings, believe me. Dirty little hussies.*" He chuckles. "*They decide who goes with who, and I daresay they sometimes swap without the Ays knowing, the big dumb apes.*"

"But don't the Ays mind all this? They're pretty proud, aren't they?"

"*Whether the girls let them think they're in charge, or whether the Ays just pretend to themselves, to save face, I don't know. But the Bees have them wrapped around their little fingers, don't you doubt it.*"

Another throaty chuckle; then his voice suddenly seems

to curdle. "*Anyway. We should get back to work. Don't go spreading round what I said there, understand?*"

"Sure."

It's the longest conversation I can ever recall having with Mr Reynolds. And now it's finished: him striding off after the Bees, and little Leila left thinking, thinking, thinking, not twenty feet away from where sister Lily choked to death as the oxygen fled her lungs.

LILY'S BURIAL TAKES place the following cycle. Two of the Overseers are there—Mr Lee and Mr Reynolds—and around ten assorted Ays, Bees and Jays. The rest are on shift, I guess. Lily is dressed in a plain tunic, and I cleaned her and washed her hair, so she looks brand new, like a virgin Ell fresh from the vats. Two Ays are carrying her on a white sheet—one of them could do it alone comfortably, but it would just look a bit odd.

In our small group, Mr Lee and I in the lead, we troop off towards the burial site. It feels like we're marching in a dignified silence, though of course any number of the group behind me could be patched in to each other, joking or muttering. After about one hundred metres, we come to the hole in the ground, marked with a metal pole. The Jays had gouged it out earlier, with some heavy-duty drills, and a mound of ore is lying to one side.

Without much ceremony, the two Ays lower Lily's body into the hole, still laid out on the sheet. Then they take shovels from their brother Alistair, and the three of them start to fill in the hole. I have to look away as a rock lands smack into my sister's face. It's not the most sensitively handled burial, compared with the ones you read about in books, but they mean well.

Soon Lily is gone, and that is that. There isn't really anything to say, and in an unspoken consensus, everyone starts to turn around at the same time, to return to the base. As I turn, I happen to glance at one of the Jays, right on my shoulder, and to my surprise I see tears filling his bloodshot eyes, and an expression of such grief that I've never seen on an Jay before—or on anyone, for that matter. We lock gazes for a moment, staring right into each other's visors, then he suddenly wrenches away, and disappears into a group with the three other Jays.

"Hey," I say, and start off after him, but the Jays mingle together as they make their way to the base, and soon I have no idea which one it was. They set a fast pace, and I hurry after them, leaving behind the others. I get through the airlock with them, but as I remove my suit, Judas approaches me and engages me in a stilted conversation of such insincerity about Lily, and how now she'll always be a part of Hell, that I nearly tell him to stop talking and get out my way. But it doesn't seem to be quite the thing to do, so I nod and thank him for his words. By the time he's finished, all the other Jays have disappeared. I'm tempted to confront him, to find out why he was blocking me from talking to one of his brothers. But that would just sound paranoid and petty, so I keep schtum.

* * *

I LIE AWAKE at dusk, failing to sleep. I try to remember Avery's burial and whether it was any different to this, but all I come up with is a foggy half-picture. I can see myself—or was it Lily?—standing at the back of a huddle, much like the one today for Lily's burial, while the Ays filled in their brother's grave. I remember noticing they had shaved off his ridiculous sideburns, and having to stifle a laugh. Did I feel any sadness at his death? I've got no special attachment to Avery or any of the Ays, but there's still a loyalty there, a bond with a fellow resident of Mizushima-00109 that is stronger than any mild personal indifference. Still, I can't imagine that I would have wept for him, the way that Jay did earlier.

I jump up, drag my cot back and look again through the gloom at the scratches. I count up the tallies of scratches again—5, 2, 2, 6. If there's a message there, I can't fathom it. My head falls back on the pillow and I softly repeat the numbers to myself, waiting for sleep to come.

5

PAWNS

I FIND JEREMY in the Leisure cabin with the chessboard laid out, practising his openings. He is the current Holder of the Board, or whatever stupid title they give themselves.

"Jeremy," I say, "I'd like to ask you a favour."

"You may ask."

"I would like—and don't freak out—to borrow your chess pieces."

He frowns. "Would you like to *challenge* me? That's the only legitimate way to take ownership of the pieces."

He delivers this completely deadpan, so I know he's probably going to relent, unless he's in a really perverse mood.

"Come on, Jeremy. You'd destroy me. I'm just asking

for a favour. Been a rough few cycles, cut me some slack?"

"Hmm. What are you going to do with them?"

"Just an experiment."

He looks dubious, no doubt contemplating the horror of being the first board-holder to lose any pieces since Rookgate, many cycles ago.

"Look, you can watch if you like. I just need to go next door. One hour, tops."

Jeremy shrugs, and carefully, piece by piece, clears the board, then piece by piece puts them into the upturned board and snaps it shut.

"Show me," he says.

The two of us walk out of Leisure and into the Community cabin. Two Bees—Brenda and Beatrice—are opening some vacuum-packed food pouches and preparing a meal. I lead Jeremy over to a table by the Rota.

"So this," I say, gesturing at the table, "is Hell."

He leans down on it, arms outstretched, like a general surveying a map. "In what way?"

"In a representative way," I say. "It's a shrunk-down icon of the asteroid. All right with you?"

He sits down on a stool next to the table. "Go on."

I go to the shelves on the wall and take a plate. "Here's the base." I put it down in the middle of the table. Next, I go to the shelves and grab three bowls. "East, North and South dig sites. Should be enough for this." They go into the three corners of the table.

"So... can you guess what I want your chessmen for?"

"You want my chessmen to be *icons*... of all of us here. The little people on your little map. But ..."

"But?"

"I don't see why you can't just use some spoons."

"Oh, come on, don't be such a sourpuss, Jeremy! The chessmen would be perfect! I'll even let you choose which piece you want to be."

He puffs out his cheeks. "Seriously? You'd let me *choose* which chess piece is going to represent me on your little map? You'd really do that for me? Earth!"

The Jays like to be sarcastic, but when there are no other Jays around to enjoy it, it falls flat.

"I will do you that honour, Jeremy."

"Go on, then." He hands over the board with a smirk. "My brothers and I can be the black pawns."

"Six black pawns," I say, counting them off, and they make a *ching* as I drop them into the plate. "And if I may, I'll be the black bishop."

"Powerful pieces, bishops," Jeremy says. "Only worth three points, but often they make the difference in the endgame."

"Yeah, yeah. Spare me the phony insights and cod psychology. They're only chess pieces."

I pick up the second black bishop, and my nerve endings tingle. "And that one," I say, "is Lily."

"Ok, I'm with you," Jeremy says after a pause. "We're going back in time, aren't we? Trying to figure out where everyone was. Deducting the identity of your sister's killer."

"Amen, brother."

I start to pick up the white pawns. "Ays? Bees?" Jeremy asks.

The two Bees look our way and giggle. I decide to make them the white pawns, and the Ays can be a mixture of white bishops, knights and the remaining rook.

"It makes sense to have Mr Lee the black king," I say, "and the other two Overseers the white king and queen."

"Rather unoriginal," says Jeremy. "But easy to remember, I suppose."

I put all the pieces on my plate, and riffle through them with my fingers. "Is that everything?"

Jeremy slides down onto the chair next to me. "Well, I don't mean to tell you your business, *Lei*," he says, staring right into my eyes, and I suddenly realise he's been trying to flirt with me; what is he playing at?

"But, if *I* were running this investigation, I'd have some icons for the jeeps. So you can figure out when we all had access to transport. And who could have got around Hell quickly."

"Okay," I say. "Yeah. Good one." I point at some coloured cups on the shelf. "Perfect."

So three cups go next to the plate—yellow, red and green to represent Banana, Tomato and Cabbage.

My map is now complete, my cast is ready, and all that is needed is to direct everyone into their correct positions. I go to the Rota archive, and pull out the sheets that started just a few cycles ago, from when I last saw Lily and she went off on shift. Piece by piece, the inhabitants of Hell are moved to where they *should* have been.

I move everything forward a few hours, and extract Aaron, Barbara and Betty from the plate, placing them into the green cup, ready for their trip to the south bowl where Alistair and Jeremy are already working. Fast forward a few hours, and Lily returns from her shift in Banana, around the same time as Tomato is heading out to East 3. Banana is carrying Lily, Mr Lee, Beatrice, Joseph and Jupiter; while Tomato has myself, Juan and Jolly, who I had that weird conversation with, plus Brenda and Bess. Mr Reynolds and Andrew were waiting for us at the East 3 site, which leaves Mr Ortiz, Andy and Ashton, Judas and Becci at the base until Lily's jeep returned.

So Lily must have disappeared sometime between this point, and nine hours later, when I returned from East 3. I check the Rota, move the clock forward four hours, when the five on the southern team returned in Cabbage.

From which I can suppose three explanations:

1) Lily went off to East 5 with her killer in Tomato before the return of Cabbage.
2) Lily went off to East 5 with her killer in Tomato or Cabbage, after the return of the southern expedition.
3) Lily went to East 5 alone, for a rendezvous at East 5 with one of my group, who dashed the few hundred metres from East 3 to East 5.

Jeremy was watching me carefully. "So?" he said. "What does it tell us?"

"Well," I say. "It tells me that pretty much anyone could, hypothetically, have had the opportunity to kill Lily. It tells me who were the last people to speak to Lily. It tells me that whoever did this had a lot of chutzpah and wasn't afraid to take a big gamble."

Jeremy sniffs and picks up the black king, rolling it between his fingers. "You want my opinion?" he says. Typically, he doesn't wait for my response. "No brother or sister is going to have done this thing. Why would one of us take the risk? You know you want to look at the Overseers. They think we're animals, freaks—they wouldn't think twice."

"I hear you, brother Jeremy. But you know what is bothering me?"

"What's bothering you, sister Leila?"

I pick up a handful of black pawns. "Identical twins. *Classic* Christie. I mean, this whole thing screams impersonation, sneaky alibis—a couple of Bees or Jays working together to have an extra pair of hands to commit the murder."

"How refreshingly open of you to discuss your accusation with the person you're accusing. Though I'm not clear what kind of trickery or impersonation you think took place."

"Neither am I, really. I'm just saying. If it *was* a couple of your brothers… I'm onto them."

"And not our dear brother Ays?"

"I suppose they *could* have—Aaron or Ashton, perhaps, swapping their glasses and cap. But…"

"But you don't think they've got the imagination."

"Frankly, no. Which doesn't preclude them committing a straightforward murder, with no trickery."

I stare at the table, my map of the asteroid, willing the clues to come out and reveal themselves. This was a great idea. A *great* idea. I totally feel like Miss Marple now (not that this was her way of solving a murder, this is more Sherlock Holmes' methods, but I never liked him). But for a moment I feel like a detective and not an Ell who's been bred to stack piles of ore.

Another Jay enters the Community cabin, and wanders over to join his brother. He raises his eyebrows at my little diorama, turns to Jeremy, and says, "Challenge."

"Ah, Judas," says Jeremy. "Somehow I knew it would be you next." He looks at me. "May I?"

I nod my assent and watch as he scoops all the pieces back into the folding board, leaving the plates and cups in position. The two Jays exit the cabin, and I follow them into the Leisure cabin. The Jays are the key to knowing what goes on in Hell, I've decided—the Overseerless, mischievous Jays—far more likely to help me than the Overseers or even the Ays and Bees.

They take their seats and start to set up the board in a desultory fashion. I perch on a crate and twiddle my thumbs. Without any ceremony or warning, Jeremy moves a white pawn forward (the Holder of the Board is always white—of course he is). Judas studies the board with furious animation.

"Listen," I say, "was there anything going on between Lily and one of your brothers?"

"Why do you ask?" Jeremy says. Judas is studying the

board, but I can feel the sudden tension in the cabin.

"Just a hunch," I say. "It's not that unlikely. They'd only be obeying their programming."

Judas snorts. "We're not robots, Leila. And—no offense—but we all know that going down that road only leads to trouble."

"Do we?" says Jeremy.

"I'm not having this fight again, brother," Judas replies. "Your Family is all you need." He toys with a pawn.

Jeremy looks sulky. "Earth knows I'm loyal to my Family. But you need to broaden your horizons, brother."

They've stopped playing chess now and Judas surveys me coldly. "This is exactly what I'm talking about. They sow dissension amongst us. They don't mean to, but they do."

"Charming," I say.

There is a glowering silence between the Jays, and then Judas makes his move. I wait for a few minutes.

"Thing is," I say, as they suddenly up their pace, exchanging a flurry of moves, "if a Jay was seeing Lily, he might know what she was up to, what was on her mind in the cycles before she was killed."

"Surely you spoke to her plenty yourself?" Jeremy says.

"I didn't see her *that* much—blame the Rota and the fact there were only two of us. And though it pains me to say it, maybe we weren't as tight as I thought—unlike your wonderful band of brothers."

Jeremy brings a knight into play. He ruffles his kinky hair, a tangle of stubby black curls. "Let me ask around. I'll see what I can find out."

Judas sighs, shakes his head. They play in silence for a while, probing, swapping a pair of pawns.

"I know you just want to find some sort of meaning in her death, Leila," Judas says. "But are you sure it wasn't just an accident, a fault with a piece of equipment? Maybe whoever was with her panicked, and thought they'd be blamed?"

"I dunno, Judas. It still leaves too many questions unanswered, like what they were doing out the base, off-Rota."

"Well, if you do find out who it was," Jeremy says, "and you need a bit of muscle, you know you can count on us. The Jays have got your back."

"Thanks, Jeremy. And what if I find out it was one of your brothers, have you got my back then?"

"I'm uniquely qualified to say it could never happen. A Jay would never kill an Ell; we couldn't do it."

I look into his brown eyes, and he stares right back, cool as you like, the beautiful bastard.

THE PACE OF the game slows to a crawl, then Judas forks both Jeremy's bishops with a knight, and regretfully, Jeremy abandons one.

Another Jay—if I had to guess, I'd say Joseph—wanders in, and after surveying the board, says to Jeremy: "C3 to E4. Surely."

"Bugger off," Jeremy murmurs. "That'd leave my left flank exposed and you know it."

"C3 to E4? What does that mean?" I say.

"It's a way to identify squares," says Judas. "The letters A to H go along the columns, and the numbers 1 to 8 up the rows. C3 is…" He drags his fingers down the rows. "There."

And that's when it hits me—what Lily was doing with the scratches. 5, 2, 2, 6. It's a reminder to herself—row 52, column 26, in the stores depot. That's how we locate all the boxes in the stores, it's a giant grid. And in a box on row 52, column 26, she had hidden… what? Something, anyway: the intruder ransacked those front boxes, trying to find it, before giving up at the scale of the task.

Lily hid it well, and in the absence of writing, left herself a scrawled tally to guide her back. Not the most secure note in cryptographic history, but good enough to baffle me at first, and I was the only other person who knew the stores grid.

I never thought chess would have any practical value, but it turns out I was wrong.

LATER, HALF-ASLEEP, I drift in and out of a dream about my sisters and me. The kind of dream that's so real that when you wake, your brain desperately tries to convince you to go back in; and when cold reality finally hits, you can't help but be cross at it. Six Ells together—Leila, Lily, Lolita, Lilith, Lara, Lucia—and where the heck did those names come from? We're in a spartan grey room, all sleek lines, and somehow I know we're in a ship, a million miles above Hell. I can't hear anything of what my sisters are saying, but it doesn't matter, I know what they mean.

And Lily's head is in Lilith's lap, and Lucia is spread-eagled out on the floor, yawning, stretching, and it's such a perfect domestic scene that I just want to weep. Most of my dreams are pretty tedious—the water purifier breaking down, or walking down never-ending rows in the ore depot. Barbara once claimed to me that she would regularly dream of Earth, though I don't get how her brain has managed to come up with an image of what Earth looks like. Especially since she's not even a big reader like me, constantly drinking in descriptions of life on the planet. But that's the Bees all over, always romanticizing Earth, even in their sleep.

Eventually, I wake up, and my brain won't let itself drag me back into the dream any more, and I remember where I am, and I remember Lily's blue lips, and my eyelashes are wet with tears. I reach beneath my bunk, take a pipe joint and angrily chuck the bastard thing at the wall.

DISORIENTATED, I MAKE my way to the Rota and I find I'm down for a work shift with Joseph and Juan. We go to East 3 together, but instead of taking Banana off to the depots, I get out with them and patch into the two Jays' channels, determined to give them a good Marpling.

"Sad, isn't it?" I say. "Now just one Ell left. Little me."

Not exactly subtle, but how *are* you supposed to start these casual 'interrogations'?

Both Jays stop adjusting their suits and turn to face me. They both make vague muttering noises of assent.

"Juan, you remember we were talking on the cycle that she died? With Jolly as well."

"*Mmm-hmm.*"

"You were telling me how you'd seen a lot of her in the last few weeks? Probably saw her more than me?"

"*Maybe.*"

"So what was her state of mind? What was she talking about?"

"*Um,*" Juan says.

"*The thing about Lily,*" Joseph says, "*was that she was always asking questions. She was convinced that something fishy was going on here. According to Lily, we weren't getting the whole truth about Mizushima or what we're doing here.*"

I nod, remembering her in our cabin when I last saw her—*something stinks here, Lei.*

"*Now, as it happens,*" Joseph continues, "*I—and my brothers—we agreed with her. But all her questions stirred things up: someone got nervy. Whereas the six of us, we're biding our time. Waiting until the right moment to strike, and then—*"

He suddenly chops through the vacuum with his glove, and I instinctively step back.

Juan cuts in on the other channel, and his voice is cold and flinty like swag. "*Everything we know— everything—comes filtered through those three men. You see the power they have? Perhaps if they were different men,*" he says, "*I'd feel more at ease, but... Reynolds: a fool. Ortiz: motivated by naked self-interest. Even Lily's precious Mr Lee—"*

"He's a good man."

"*As your sister told me. Maybe you're both right. But, behind his preening words... I don't trust him.*"

"So what do we do?"

"*There are eighteen of us, and three of them,*" says Joseph. "*When the time is right, we will brush them off like ore dust from our boots. But until them, we wait, we prepare, and we get the information we need.*"

A hundred metres away, two figures appear from the tunnels, dragging trolleys. From their size, they look like Ays. They stop and stare at us, our trio clustered around Banana. I raise a hand in tentative greeting, but they do not respond. Joseph turns his back on me, and heads towards them with bouncing steps. "*Stay strong, sister,*" his voice says, as his figure retreats.

Juan grips my arm and squeezes so hard I nearly cry out.

I'm unsettled, and I sit in Banana for a few minutes, not moving. I've never seen any of the Jays like that before, so serious, so intense. It's kind of attractive.

I mentally thank Lily for somehow turning the Jays into such loyal allies—though there's a nagging voice at the back of my head: this could be a textbook gambit, a killer getting close to the detective—hello, *Death in the Clouds*—pretending to help when in fact they're getting the juicy inside story on how the investigation is progressing...

Just the kind of sneaky double-bluff that the chess-playing Jays would appreciate. I can't trust *anyone*.

I glance over towards the Ays, and see they've been joined by an Overseer, probably Ortiz, with a stripe down his suit. I mull over what Joseph was saying: eighteen of us, and three of them. I know he's right, we could take over the asteroid easily. A co-ordinated attack and we'd overwhelm them, tasers or no tasers. A question mark hangs over the Ays: would they take part in any glorious revolution? There's a danger that they—bovine, incurious—would be resistant to regime change (if that's not too grand a phrase to describe the situation). I can imagine them choosing to side with the status quo. A scene pops into my head from nowhere—some Jays and some Ays arguing about this very scenario; the Jays urging them on, the Ays in almost-comic horror at the outrage of what they're suggesting.

Ah, revolution, revolution. I realise I've let myself be dragged along by the fervour of the Jays' plans and whispers. And yet, despite everything, I don't even think I could go along with them. Two objections: One, Mr Lee. They have him wrong, and I want to be on his side. Two, the Collection Ship. In six hundred cycles, it is coming, revolution or not. And our passage to Earth depends on there being no bloody revolts or general misbehaviour. Just for a moment, the thought flits across my mind of somehow repelling the Collection Ship, rejecting Earth, setting up our own peaceful little community here on Hell.

But then I realise what a ridiculous idea that is. For one thing, what would we *do*? With no Rota or purpose for existence, how would we fill our time, in a way that doesn't include chipping away at pieces of now-worthless swag?

We're in a bind. Hell needs Earth more than Earth needs Hell. And without the Collection Ship, and the crates of swag accumulating in the depot, all we are is a piece of rock floating inconsequentially through space.

6

THREE EXHIBITS

THERE ARE PILES of swag in the ore depot, waiting to be sorted, but frankly, I don't give a monkey's (sometimes Mr Lee laughs when I use phrases like that, especially the more colourful ones; I don't even know what a blooming monkey looks like). Instead, I go to the stores depot, whispering Lily's numbers to myself as I walk: "Fifty-two, twenty-six."

Short of carving Lily's tally into my skin, it's the best way to remember. There are only forty rows in our grid, which is how I know 52 must refer to the columns. So I stride up to column 52, past the opened crates and mess, still untouched after three cycles; past the shelves of pipes and hardware and mesh. I turn into the grid and make for row 26, not even having to count now, instinct taking me to the intersection.

I stop and look around. Nothing's jumping out at me. I reach out to feel a random crate, but the lid's seal is tight. What am I supposed to do, Lily, open up every crate in the sector? I slump down on a corner crate, and the lid wobbles...

Hello.

I slide the lid off, and immediately it's clear this is the one I want. It's half-empty: plastic food pouches packed into the bottom half, and on top of them three items, which I lift out gingerly for inspection.

Exhibit A: Ashton's glasses. Boy. That is not what I was expecting to find.

Exhibit B: A torn half-page of the Rota, nothing remarkable about it at first glance; looks like any other page of the Rota, except that it's torn in half (sacrilege!) A gimp like Mr Ortiz would probably be able to take one look and tell me its significance, but I'm stumped. I take a quick look at what Lily was scheduled to do during the five cycles covered by the page, and what I was scheduled to do, but... nothing of particular interest.

Exhibit C: A small photograph, just a few inches high and wide, of a woman. The acetate is creased, and one corner is folded over. The colour is faded, and it looks as though it's been fingered a lot. Exhibits A and B, I know where they're from, even if I don't get their meaning yet. But this—what was Lily doing with a photograph of what appears to be a woman from Earth? Presumably, it belongs to one of the Overseers. I can't think how else it got here.

She is... beautiful.

I thought the Bees were beautiful, but this woman is something else. Perfectly symmetric face, laughter lines circling her eyes, epic cheek bones. I get it now, when you read about beauty in books, and the lengths some men go to for it. It's not posed, the photo, but looks as though she's seated somewhere, holding a mug with a garish logo. She doesn't seem to be aware she's being photographed—or if she is, she's acting as though she's not.

I rummage around the rest of the pouches, but they are packed tight, and that, it seems, is that. Lily's little treasure trove. What was she collecting them for? The thought occurs to me that those three little items may have somehow contributed to her death, and I feel sick in my gut.

There is nothing more to be done for the moment. I decide that the glasses and photo are safest here—there's nothing more they can tell me if I take them to the base. The Rota half-page, however, I take with me—a bit of study might wrinkle out its secret. I fold it and re-fold and secrete it within my suit, then seal the crate and exit the stores depot, leaving behind the mess and the unsorted swag. Banana is waiting, and another sluggish sunrise is taking place ahead, to announce a new cycle. It's time to talk to Mr Lee.

* * *

BACK AT THE base, I knock on his door without checking the Rota. He's less sociable than the other two Overseers, and often to be found in his cabin. The sound of shuffling and cursing, then: "Who is it?"

"Leila."

He comes to the door, and I see I've woken him, but he doesn't seem bothered. "Can't sleep," he says. "Come in."

He takes two sachets and prepares some tea. It is odourless and bland, even by Hell's standards, but I accept it, as I know he likes it.

"So," he says, "how's the investigation coming along?"

He makes no mention of the fact I should be working at the depots right now, but whether out of ignorance or sympathy I don't know. I sip my tea and tell him about my conversations with Mr Ortiz, Mr Reynolds and the Jays. I make no mention of Lily's message, or the three items she hid in a crate. Why, I'm not quite sure; maybe part of my brain has let Juan's hints about Mr Lee worm their way in. But also I feel like this is just mine, the only thing I've got left of my sister. And until I've figured out what it means, I'm not sharing it with anyone. (Of course, it could mean Lily's a raving kleptomaniac. Every missing chisel, trinket and spoon from the last couple of orbits could be hidden away in assorted crates. I hope it's not that.)

Mr Lee asks the right questions, makes the right noises.

"What have Mr Reynolds and Mr Ortiz said?" I ask.

He gives a tight smile. "All of the Overseers support you and want you to get to the bottom of this."

"I'm not sure Mr Ortiz does," I say.

"Don't you worry about Mr Ortiz. His bark is worse than his bite."

"Really?"

"I'm sure of it. So who next? You're going to talk to the Ays and the Bees?"

I nod. "Before that, though, can I ask you a few things?"

"Be my guest."

"So… do you remember driving back to base with Lily, the cycle before she died?"

"Yup. With Beatrice and… a couple of Jays, I think."

"Right. So, did you see her again, or was that the last time?"

"The last time. I went back to my cabin, exhausted, slept for eight hours straight. Then I was up writing and reading in my cabin, until you came to me."

"Okay. And how did she seem in the jeep? Did you talk to her?"

"Yes, she was… full of energy, buzzing with questions and ideas."

"Like what?"

"Well, out of nowhere, she kept asking me about Overseer Fedorchuk, and how he died, and whether or not the Jays had liked him. She was trying to get me to say if I thought they'd killed him. All this, mind you, with two Jays sitting next to me in the jeep."

"And what did you tell her?"

"It was… a long time ago. Very early days on the colony. He just got sick, and a few cycles later, he was dead. Back on Earth, he would have gone straight to a doctor, and I'm sure they would have fixed him up in no time. Here, we don't have that luxury."

"But the Jays are programmed with medical knowledge, aren't they?"

"They are," he admits. "But only at a basic level. Perhaps they could have done more—but nothing could have been proved. I was busy at the time, not involved— all I know is that none of the Jays had been able to figure out what was wrong. Sometimes, you're just sick, and there's nothing you can do about it."

"So you told Lily all this?"

"Yup. I was hoping to steer her away, telling her it was a non-story, but… you know Lily. Well, you know *you*. She wanted to find out more."

"Is there any way someone in the jeep could have been listening in? Joseph or Jupiter? Or Beatrice?"

He shrugs. "I didn't hear another channel cutting in, but then I wasn't listening for it."

"Okay—fast forward to when you're in your cabin afterwards. Do you remember hearing anyone walk past your door to the airlock?"

"I do remember hearing footsteps going past, but no voices."

"When was this?"

"Quite late on—just a few hours before you came to me."

Interesting. Very interesting. I wish I had my diorama now. Bloody Jays and their chess.

"The bugger here," I say to Mr Lee, "is proving

anything. I mean, suppose I figure out who killed her. But how to prove it, when everyone has a ready-made alibi? Okay—not you Overseers—but the rest, they can all get a brother or sister to say they were with them, any time they want."

"Right," says Mr Lee, "but you've got to think of motive, means, opportunity. If you can't prove means or opportunity, you've got to focus on motive. Figure that out, then…"

"Then what? The classic gambit—trick them into making a confession?"

"Could do. Or just confront them. See what happens."

We sit in silence for a while.

"Do you know if Lily was sleeping with any of the Jays?" I ask. "We saw each other so on-and-off—it would have been easy for her to do it without me knowing."

"Possible. There's a programmed attraction between Jays and Ells. If it wasn't for the… imbalance, you would have all paired off at the start. What makes you ask?"

I tell him about the crying Jay at Lily's funeral. "Part of me thinks he could help me. He'll want to find Lily's killer too, right? But then Mr Ortiz reckons that makes them a suspect, that sex is at the root of all murders."

"Hmm."

"What do you think, should I trust them?"

Mr Lee looks at me carefully, does that little tic where he scratches below his ear. "If you're right, and a Jay *was* having a relationship with Lily, then I think we can trust him to want to find the killer, as much as we do. But that doesn't rule out a different Jay killing her, as a result of the relationship. And regardless, don't forget one thing— the Jays are in it for the Jays. They'll do what's best for them—and to hell with the consequences."

Normally I'm dog-tired after a shift and fall asleep straightaway, but I didn't do much work (beyond Marpling away and hunting for clues). So I'm still awake. And it's these times, when I can't sleep, that I get rare memories of the early cycles floating through my mind. There's a dull throb in my head, but I don't mind—I ignore it and enjoy the memory.

We were in the Community cabin—me, Barbara, Bess, Andy and Avery, this must have been before his burial under a pile of ore. I had heard raised voices and wandered in to see what was happening (I mean, I'm not nosy, but do you have any idea how little goes on in this place?).

Barbara and Bess were together, Barbara perched on the arm of Bess' chair. Andy and Avery were standing, arguing.

"You must have known!" Avery was saying. "You're not stupid, you knew it wasn't her!"

They were right in each other's faces, it was fascinating— you don't often get such direct confrontations in our community. Pretty quickly, I picked up the gist of the argument: that Andy had slept with Barbara, who was Avery's girl. According to Andy, unwittingly; he claimed he had thought it was Betty, his girl, and that Barbara had deceived him. Avery, from the look on his face, remained sceptical.

Barbara, of course, was watching all this posturing with a sideways smile. The Ays weren't really paying her or Bess any attention.

So, you know, not the most original story of all time. But hey, it was a little piece of drama for our small colony, and I'm sure I later dissected it gleefully with Lily. As I remember, it didn't actually explode into a full fight— but they were squaring up to each other, and if one had crossed a line and manhandled his brother, it would have degenerated into a brawl.

I think it just fizzled out—I can remember Avery making a *tcha* noise of disgust, shoving past Andy and storming out without a glance at the Bees. Andy made a vague, exasperated *what-is-his-problem?* gesture at the cabin, and then went next door to the Leisure cabin.

What did I do then? It would have been too awkward, surely, to talk to the Bees about what just happened— or to talk about anything else, as though nothing had happened. Surely? I mean, social conventions are pretty slapdash here on Hell, but there are some instincts you just can't ignore.

I probably gave the Bees an embarrassed look, eyebrows raised, and backed out of the Community cabin. Probably. The memory doesn't go on that far, anyway. But it's a good memory, the details are clear, and seeing Avery again is an unexpected bonus. When I get a memory like that, I like to hoard it and polish it like a precious gemstone. And I'll revisit it again and again, until I'm not remembering the memory, but the narrative I've told myself of the memory. Does that make sense? Like when I've read a good book, and I'll give Mr Lee the gist of the story. And it stops being *the* story and becomes *my* story.

I NEED TO interview the Bees. As it happens, they come to me. I am in my cabin, three hours before my next shift, when Brenda's head pokes around the door.

"Leila," she says. "When are you going to talk to us?"

"What do you—?"

"Everyone's talking about it. How you're going round *grilling* the whole colony. But you haven't done any of us yet."

"Well—would now be okay?"

"Of course—we're waiting for you in our cabin."

We walk the short journey through the tunnels, from my cabin to theirs. Brenda offers me her hand, and my fingers slot into hers. I can't help but be reminded of walking these tunnels with Bess, as we trundled behind Messrs Lee and Reynolds, hunting for Lily.

I dart a glance at Brenda's silky brown hair, and reassess my comparison of the Bees with the woman in the photograph. She was beautiful, true, but it was a beauty that looked as if it'd been designed by a computer. The Bees (who, to some extent, *were* designed by computer), have a more real, raw, imperfect—yes, Hell-ish—beauty. I do love little ironies like that: they make life worthwhile.

Brenda pushes open the door of her cabin, and in we go. I haven't been in here for a while. Hasn't changed since last time, but what do you expect? Bess and Beatrice are sitting on their bunks, cross-legged. Brenda sits down with me, and squeezes my hand. "Here we are, then," she says. "Just us girls together."

I try to smile back at her. The Bees always make me feel clumsy and awkward, especially when I'm with more than one of them.

"So," says Bess, "what are you going to ask us about?"

"Um..." I say, "Beatrice—you were with Lily in Banana, weren't you, driving back to base? It was a few hours before she died."

"Yes, I remember," Beatrice says.

"How did she seem? Did you talk to her or anything?"

"Sorry, I didn't talk to her. And with hoods on, you don't get much idea how anyone's feeling."

"Was she talking to anyone else?"

"I think to Mr Lee a bit. Then we arrived here, and she was first off, hurried inside. I never saw her again."

"And Brenda," I say, "you were out in East 3 with me. Did you see anything weird, anyone doing anything unexpected?"

She shakes her head. "We were out taking measurements the whole time, with Reynolds. He wandered off once, he said to check how the Jays were getting on, came back about an hour later."

"Okay, Bess," I say, changing tack. "You're with Ashton, right? Do you know why he wears glasses?"

For the first time, the Bees look baffled.

"His glasses?" Bess says. "You know, they like to distinguish themselves from each other."

"Right—but... any reason why *he* has glasses in particular?"

"I have no idea."

"All I mean is—"

"Leila," Brenda interrupts, at my side. "Have you got a plan ready? For when you catch the killer?"

"Not exactly," I say, thinking of Mr Ortiz, sneering at me with his *where's the prison* and his *little jury*.

"We're not on Earth yet," Brenda says. "You can't expect Earth justice here."

"What are you saying?"

"This is a frontier land. So frontier justice."

"And if you find him," says Beatrice, "you'd better get your justice in first. Because he wouldn't hesitate to kill you, if he's already killed Lily."

"He?"

"Oh, come on, Leila," says Beatrice. All three Bees are leaning forward now, and I feel a rush of happiness at being part of this gang, and also a pang of regret for my five missing sisters. "It wasn't a Bee, you can guarantee that. We girls have to stand together. I don't know which of them it was—a Jay, maybe, or an Overseer—but you make sure you're ready, to do what you have to do."

"But how?" I say. "I don't have any weapons. How could I do anything to hurt one of them?"

Beatrice grins. "There's weapons everywhere," she says. "Look at your poor sister's hood. You just have to find them."

"Can you help me?" I ask in a small voice.

"Find out who it is first," says Brenda. "If it's an Ay, you can hardly expect us to help. But anyone else—you come to us, we'll help you out."

I should have interrogated everyone ages ago. Fascinating, some of the stuff you unearth. I want to ask them how they handle the 6-Bees-to-5-Ays conundrum, which is embarrassing, but I'm already embarrassed by the whole situation, so I plunge in: "Do you remember Avery?"

Brenda looks amused. "Avery? Of course, how could we not? We see his brothers every cycle."

"Sure—but just a few hours ago, I was trying to sleep, and I had this clear memory of him and Andy having an argument. About Barbara. Avery was saying Andy had slept with her, but Andy claimed she had tricked him."

"You'd have to ask her," Brenda says.

"You were there," I say to Bess. "Do you remember?"

"Memories," says Bess. "I wouldn't put too much faith in *memories*, Leila. Don't blindly believe what you *think* you remember, or what *they* tell you. The only things you can trust are right in front of your eyes."

She shuffles towards me, on her haunches, and reaches out a long, pale arm. She grabs my ankle.

"This is solid truth, Leila, right here." She shuffles nearer, and puts a palm on my left cheek. "And this. The only reality you can put your faith in."

I'm sat in a sandwich of Bees. The tension in the cabin is excruciating—the air around me seems twice as dense as before.

"Right," I say. "Got it. Truth. Reality. But—and I don't want to be too literal-minded—some things you can't reach out and touch. I mean, that's why I'm asking everyone questions."

The three Bees smile back at me blankly. Bess purses her lips, and I notice Brenda has too.

"How does it work?" I say. "What I'm trying to say is, how does it work, with you and the Ays? Six of you, five of them. I just want to know. Maybe it doesn't matter— you can say it's none of my business."

"We manage," Bess says, stroking my arm.

Seriously, no one on this bloody colony is capable of giving a straight answer.

7

NAUGHTY

EITHER I'M VERY gullible or everyone else is very convincing. Every time I interrogate someone, I end up changing my mind. I spoke to the Jays, and ended up convinced that an Overseer had killed Lily, and we were all going to rise up in revolution against them. But half an hour with the Bees, and my suspicions have fallen on the Jays; and I'm examining cutlery in the Community cabin, weighing up whether I could use a blunted knife to get vigilante justice.

At that moment, a Jay enters, carrying a sheaf of instructions. I drop the knife back in the drawer.

"Hello," he says. "Jolly here."

"Yeah," I say, wandering over to the Rota. The torn

half-page is pressed against my hip inside my boiler suit, but I don't need to bring it out yet. All I need to do is find its match—a torn half page in the archive. What that will tell me, Earth knows: if there was anything interesting in it, why didn't Lily rip the whole page out? So there must be some sign, some reminder, which will explain what my sister was up to. I flick through the pages, hundreds of pages, slowly so I don't miss what I'm looking for. I can feel Jolly's eyes on me.

It really is a staggeringly dull record of our lives on Hell, little black marks in little black and white squares, non-stop movement from base to sites to base. A giant, tedious chessboard, with no checkmate ever in sight.

Nice. I like the analogy, and nearly share it with Jolly.

The lines and marks are beginning to blur, and I have to blink hard twice to stay awake. I'm starting to get concerned—there's no sign of any torn page, which doesn't really make sense. I slow right down for the last fifty pages, but... nothing.

Curious. Very curious. All I can assume is that the other half was ripped out too. But by whom? By Lily, and hidden in a second stash somewhere in the depot? Why separate them, though? Or had somebody else already ripped out that half, and Lily just took the second half to find its twin?

I start again, riffling through the pages, figuring that I must have missed it during my blurry 'chessboard' moment. At that point, Mr Ortiz and two Ays—Aaron and Alistair—come in. Ays are just what I want to see, my last interviewees, but these are the wrong ones. I need to talk to Ashton, the owner of the glasses that Lily decided to nick; and Andrew, who was cross about Lily sticking her nose into the Ays' business.

The three men are grimy, they look exhausted, even Mr Ortiz. They start to prepare some food, and Mr Ortiz sends a sour look in my direction.

"What are you doing with the archive, girlie?" he says.

"Just checking where everyone was when Lily was killed," I reply.

"Why are you halfway through the archive, then? You should be on the top page."

The two Ays have stopped to watch, and Jolly pipes up from his corner: "What is this, classified information? Do we have to get permission to read about our own movements now?"

Mr Ortiz jabs a finger in Jolly's direction. "You want to fucking watch it, mister." There are bright red spots on his cheeks, visible among the stubble and dust.

"Watch what?"

"We've let things get way too lax here," Mr Ortiz says. "There's going to be a reckoning, mark my words."

"Take it easy," Jolly says.

"You don't tell me to take it easy. One of these cycles, I'll wipe the smirk off your face, off all your runty little Jay faces."

Jolly is impassive. Mr Ortiz snatches up his pouches, and leaves the Community cabin. The Ays return to their food, and I mouth *thank you* to Jolly, though he is engrossed in his instruction manuals again.

I wander over to talk to Aaron, in the baseball cap. "What's up with him?" I ask.

"Damn Jays," Aaron says, glaring at Jolly. "Always stirring the pot, causing problems."

Ays and Jays have the most dysfunctional relationship on the asteroid. It's not hard to see why. To the Ays, the Jays are beta males who have to use machinery instead of their muscles; they're the weasel-tongued charmers who make the Bees laugh; they're the unruly mavericks who laugh at the Ays and wound their pride. Out in the tunnels, they work together reasonably well—in silence, but slotting together in their different roles. But here on the base, they steer well clear of each other. It's another reason why a rebellion is implausible—I don't think they could ever put aside their mutual dislike.

"Still," I say. "Mr O's not usually in quite such a cranky mood."

Alistair, clearing away the rubbish of his pouches, speaks: "A lot of funny things going on lately. Mr Ortiz doesn't like it."

A snort from Jolly in the corner, which Alistair ignores.

"Funny things?" I say.

"Your sister, for one thing," Alistair says bluntly. "I know you're the most upset by it—but the rest of us are worried too."

"See, our brother's death," Aaron chimes in, "no doubt that was an accident. Sad, but not worrying. Someone killing your sister, though—that's worrying."

"Right," I say. "Well, you can tell Mr Ortiz that's why I'm asking all these questions—I'm trying to solve this."

Aaron grunts.

"Okay," I say. "So what other funny things?"

"Things going missing," Alistair says. "A place this size, shouldn't happen. Mr Ortiz—not happy."

"What, his taser?"

"Yeah, his taser. But you've also got Ashton's glasses. Who would steal a pair of glasses?"

Awkward.

"And Mr Reynolds' key," Aaron says. "Went missing for two cycles. Funny things going on. I don't like it either."

I didn't know about *that*. "What do you mean, two cycles? It just went missing, then reappeared?"

"He just found the key again in his boiler suit. But I saw him searching that boiler suit with my own eyes, when he first lost it, in the airlock—and it wasn't there, no way."

"When was this?"

"Seven or eight cycles ago," he says. "Mr Reynolds, he was just relieved to find it again. But Mr Ortiz... it worries him."

"What exactly are you boys so worried about?" Jolly says, rising from his chair and wandering over. "Big lads like you, running scared 'cause a few things have gone missing?"

Aaron gives him a scornful look. "Good Earth—we ain't scared of anything, pretty boy," he says. "All I know is we got to sit tight for six hundred cycles, hold it together. And we don't need you, or anyone else, stirring the pot."

For once, nobody seems inclined to stomp out at this point in the argument. So the three of them get back to what they were doing, in a simmering, angry silence.

In the meantime, I check the Rota, to find out where Ashton and Andrew are—my last two interviewees. Both are on a work shift—Ashton will be back in four hours, Andrew in eight hours. I make my way back to my cabin, and bump into Mr Lee in the spine tunnel.

"Leila," he says. "Mr Reynolds isn't too happy about the amount of swag that's piling up in the depot. I know it's been difficult lately, but it might be a good idea to keep him quiet, no?"

"I'm sorry, I..."

"Look, how about the two of us go now? Make a start on it together? We'll have to make some changes to the Rota, with just one Ell—everyone will have to pitch in to help you. But for now, this will keep people happy."

I agree—I've got four hours to kill before Ashton's return. So the two of us, we go to the airlock, we suit up and climb on board Cabbage. We get to the depots, and Mr Lee doesn't make a big deal about the work: he just gets on with it, sorting and lifting and packing crates. The time passes slowly. I'm thinking about what the Ays said, and how there's a lot going on here that I don't know about, bubbling under the surface. And really, it's a surprise we don't have more fights and what Mr Lee would call "unpleasant scenes."

In a way, it's quite a relief to get back to the mindless work. Lately, it's been too much excitement for me to handle. The grief, the drama, the conspiracies: that's why I've been buzzing the whole time and unable to go to sleep. There's a thought—I used to pride myself on how placid I was, how I could let my mind go blank. Is that just 'cause I was bored out my bloody mind, tranquilised to within an inch of my life?

Well, regardless, a bit of tedious sorting is just what I need right now. A comedown from the last few cycles. And occasionally, my gloves scrape against serrated rock edges or my arms strain at the weight of a crate, and it reminds me I'm alive.

With Mr Lee's help, the depot is looking in a much better state after a few hours; there's still a lot of testing to be done, but superficially it's a big improvement, certainly enough to keep Mr Reynolds happy. I plead tiredness after a few hours, and Mr Lee takes me back to the Base. Banana is already back, which means Ashton is too. I de-suit, and make my way to the Ays' cabin, where Ashton is getting ready for a sleep shift.

"Ashton," I say. "Can I have a word?"

"All right," he says. "But not a long one. I'm knackered."

"Thanks—so what I want to know is: what happened to your glasses?"

"My glasses? I thought this was supposed to be all questions about Lily?"

"It might be. It's a curious event, no clear explanation."

Ashton looks at me critically. "Are you sure you're cut out for this, Leila?"

"Is it possible you lost the glasses off-base?"

"Nope. I always take them off when I suit up, and leave them in the airlock with my other clothes. That's when someone must have nicked them."

"But why steal glasses? Who would do that?"

"Come on, Leila," he says. "Who likes practical jokes? Who doesn't need a good reason for anything? It was one of the Jays, wasn't it? Trying to wind me up."

I know it wasn't the Jays—but maybe it's not the glasses per se that were important to Lily, they were a means to an end: a reminder, pointing to Ashton, to say… what exactly? Is this the killer in front of me?

"Go back a few cycles," I tell him. "Just before Lily died. You were here on the base, weren't you?"

"If the Rota says so."

"You can't remember?"

Ashton sighs, and clasps together two meaty hands. This close, I can see all the bruises and cuts that freckle his arms. "I don't know about you," he says, "but I go on shift, I dig some swag, I pull it out. I come back to base and recover, I relax. Then I go and dig some more swag. One cycle is pretty much the same as any other."

"But there's got to be more to it than that," I say. "Otherwise, what's the point of living at all?"

"I'll leave that question to the philosophers." He must sense my frustration, because he puts a hand on my forearm (a thin, jaundiced twig, dwarfed by his olive-brown fingers). "Look, Leila," he says gruffly. "I know you must be hurting 'cause of your sister. I lost a brother too, remember? But all we got to do is sit tight for the next six hundred cycles. We don't want anyone stirring the pot, you know?"

It is the exact same phrase Aaron used. Is it a line that Mr Ortiz fed to them all, or have they come up with it themselves, parroting it to each other in the echo chamber of the Ays' simple world?

Who cares—the point is, there must be a reason why Lily singled out this Ay, and stole his glasses as a memo, to draw a big red circle around him. What's so special about him?

"You're with Bess, aren't you, Ashton?" I ask.

"Yep."

"You ever been with any of the others?"

He frowns. "Earth, no. I wouldn't do that to my brothers."

"All right, then."

"Are we finished?"

I guess we are.

So NEXT UP is Andrew. I pass the time waiting for him to return in my cabin, not feeling in the mood for the company of whoever might be in the Community or Leisure cabins. I have taken to sleeping in Lily's bunk, and I rest there now, swaddling myself in the blankets. There's a vague Lily-smell here, a kind of fustiness that is not unpleasant. I lie there, motionless, eyes flickering around as I try to spot some other sign Lily left—maybe marks scrawled on the ceiling or the bunk.

I'm filled with a sudden glow of pride for my clever sister. Someone thought they could silence her by ripping off her hood, but she was too canny for them. She hid these things where they couldn't be found, and left me a message, from the grave.

I'm not an idiot. I know that going down this path, following in her footsteps, could put me in the same danger. But I'd rather be on that path than the one where I shrug, idly wonder who killed my sister, and return to not stirring the pot on Hell.

I HEAR THE footsteps in the spine tunnel when Andrew's party returns from their shift. I rise from Lily's bunk, and when the clatter has died down, I go the Ays' cabin. Ashton is asleep in there, and I gesture to Andrew. He frowns, and comes out to the synthetic tunnel. I haven't spoken to him since looking for Lily's body together.

"What's the matter?" he says.

"I need to speak with you, Andrew. How about we go to the airlock?"

He doesn't move. "What about?"

"I need to know what Lily was pestering you lot about. You remember, you told me to tell her to back off from the Ays' business?"

"Oh, that." We are standing in the tunnel, and I'm conscious of our conversation echoing down into the spine. "Look, Leila, if you want my advice, don't—"

"If you tell me not to stir the pot," I say, "I swear

I'll take a fork and stab you in the eye. I get it—no pot-stirring. If you help me, I might be able to stop the person who *is* stirring."

"I wasn't going to say that," he says, looking hurt (but I think he was).

"Oh."

"The Ays have always respected the Ells," he says. "The Bees are our girls, but we respect the Ells. We just don't want you to get hurt."

"That sounds like a threat."

"It's not," he snaps. "Look, Lily was asking everyone questions, not just us. If you must know, she was asking about Avery, and how he died; she was asking about Ashton and whether we trusted him, for goodness' sake!"

"Okay."

"Our own brother! Anyway, she was doing the same thing to the Bees and the Jays—my advice was that she back off before she asked someone the wrong question."

"Or the right one," I said. "Do you know what was making her suspicious of Ashton?"

"I do not. If she was suspicious of him, she should have been suspicious of me too. Of all of us. But the Ays ain't got nothing to hide."

"Two last questions, Andrew. Remind me, who's your girl?"

"It's Becci."

"And the cycle Lily died, you were on East 3, weren't you? It was the same time you spoke to me about Lily."

"If you say so."

"Do you remember seeing anything strange—anyone acting unusually?"

He pauses for a moment. "Only that I saw an Overseer walking down by the tunnels, away from East 3. Grey stripe on his suit. Couldn't tell who at that distance."

"Why was that unusual?"

"Just that no Overseer had any business down by the tunnels right then. Mr Reynolds was the only one in the East zone, but he was supposed to be up on the ridge, with the Bees. Strange."

I'VE FINISHED MY interviews, and already I know what my next step is. The photograph in Lily's stash has been nagging at me. Logically, the only place it could have come from is one of the Overseers' cabins. Since they are locked, all I could think was that she'd seen it in Mr Lee's cabin, and distracted him while she took it. But after speaking to the Ays, a far more likely scenario presents itself—that she was the one who stole Mr Reynolds' key, and had a hunt around his cabin. Only... it wouldn't be her, would it? I couldn't imagine myself picking his pocket, so Lily couldn't either. But the Jays... I could picture those nimble-fingered scamps doing it without so much as breaking a sweat. And if Lily had been sleeping with a Jay, there's your explanation for why they might have given the key to her.

When I get to their cabin, a Jay is sitting on his bunk, fiddling with his hair. Another is asleep on his bunk. I raise a questioning eyebrow, and the Jay says, "Jeremy." He cocks his head at his sleeping brother. "Jupiter."

"Jeremy," I say in a low voice, and close the door. "We need to talk."

"Mmm-hmm?"

"Before she died, Lily made a reference to finding something in Mr Reynolds' cabin." (She hadn't, of course. But I wasn't about to reveal the clues she left me, even if the Jays *were* on my side.) "I didn't understand at the time, but then earlier I heard about Mr Reynolds' key going missing for two cycles. One of you stole it, and gave it to her, didn't you?"

Jeremy doesn't say anything, but there is a half-smile creeping on the corner of his lips, and I know he wants to admit to it. "What makes you say that?" he says eventually.

"Please, Jeremy. I'm right, aren't I? Come on, whatever obligation you had to Lily should carry over to me—I am her sister. I just want to see what she saw—take a look around his cabin."

Jeremy tuts and shakes his head. "Naughty, little sister. That would be very naughty. You trying to stir the pot?"

A movement makes me glance to my right, and I see that Jupiter is now awake, studying me, his head resting on upturned palms.

"I said it was a mistake," he says to Jeremy. "All along, I said it."

"You admit it, then? You let Lily into his cabin?"

"Maybe. But we don't have to make the same mistake again. Look what happened to Lily—we don't want that to happen to you, do we?"

"I'm ready this time. Damn it, you have to do this. You owe it to Lily. Please!"

"Even if, as you say, we helped Lily," Jupiter says, "what makes you think we *could* help you out now? Mr Reynolds found the key in his suit, didn't he?"

"But if I know you Jays right," I say, "the only reason you would have returned the key is if it was a bluff to make him think the cabin was safe again."

"Meaning?"

"You made a copy, didn't you?"

Jeremy shrugs and laughs at his brother. "She's got it all figured out, hasn't she?" They look at each other, and a silent conversation seems to be taking place.

"We should let her," Jeremy says. "It might be a catalyst for further developments. We can keep an eye out for her."

"You're making a mistake, brother," Jupiter says, climbing down from his bunk. "I won't join you in it, and neither will our brothers."

Disagreement amongst the Jays. I can't decide if this is a good thing or a bad thing.

"We've become complacent," Jeremy says. "How do we get anywhere unless we take some risks? We're blind men right now, none of us daring to leave the safety of what we know."

"Blind, but alive," Jupiter says.

"I don't see why you won't just help me," I say. "We're all in this together."

Jupiter turns to me, comes up close, and gives me the deadest stare you can imagine. "You talk of blind men," he says to Jeremy, still staring at me. "But we've allowed ourselves to be blinded by these Ells. Sure, they look like pretty, harmless things. But they're dangerous. Her sister, she could have brought us all down with her. This one, she'll do the same."

"And what's *that* supposed to mean?" I say.

But he turns on his heel and walks out, insolently slow.

"This is on you," is his parting shot to his brother. "You show her, it's on you."

"What's his problem?" I say.

"Not all my brothers are as enlightened as me," he replies, but he sounds distracted.

"What's the deal, then? Are you going to show me, or are you going to let him tell you what to do?"

Jeremy smiles. "Nice try. But there's no need. Come on, let's check on the Rota for Mr Reynolds' whereabouts, then we'll do this."

MR REYNOLDS, IT turns out, is sitting in the Community cabin as we walk in—sprawled by the windows, dully staring out at space. I freeze, but Jeremy greets him, cool as you like, and walks up to the Rota. He scans it, nods, smiles at Barbara who is sat on the opposite side of the cabin to Mr Reynolds, and walks out with me.

"Great," he says. "He's off in just over two hours. An eight-hour shift in the South sector. Mr Lee's out too."

"So where's the key?" I say.

"Patience."

"You can tell me how this all happened with Lily, at least."

"I was hardly involved. Some of my brothers handled it. But I know she came to us, asking if it was possible to break into the Overseers' cabins. Jolly had spotted that Mr Reynolds was pretty careless with his key, so we gave it a shot. Jolly picked his pocket with no problems, then Juan made a thin duplicate using a sheet of aluminium—took a few tries to cut the teeth right, but it worked eventually. They let Lily in while Mr Reynolds was out, and locked her in, while they kept an eye on the spine. Then after half an hour, they let her out. She seemed satisfied."

"Did she say anything?"

"As I say, I wasn't there myself."

"Which of you was?"

"I... don't know, Leila. What I suggest is we do the same for you—let you in, then let you out after you've had a chance to rummage around."

I agree before he has a chance to change his mind or speak to the other Jays. He guides me back to my cabin and shows me an old drill that has been abandoned there for a while. He unscrews the back, and removes the casing to show the thin duplicate key—jagged and rough, but a key nonetheless.

"Meet me at Reynolds' cabin, an hour after he leaves."

The wait is intolerable. All I can think about is what I'm going to find in Mr Reynolds cabin. I mean, I know what Lily found, but there's got to be more to it than that, or why would Lily have taken it? I cannot daydream, or relax, or go to the Community cabin where Mr Reynolds is. I cannot face the stares and chatter that will be found in the Leisure cabin. I sit on my bunk and fume.

TWO HOURS LATER, I walk briskly up the spine and soon hear Jeremy's footsteps a few paces behind me. Of course, if this were a double-cross, now would be a perfect opportunity to kill me and dump my body in Mr Reynolds' cabin. There's a thought. But I've read too many hammy thrillers. There is not going to be a double-cross.

We reach Mr Reynolds' door. I glance around, and Jeremy has his finger on his lips. Mr Ortiz could easily be just twenty metres away in his cabin. Jeremy slots the makeshift key into the lock, turns the pins with a *scree*, and pushes open the door for me. In I go, and he closes the door behind me with a gentle *click*.

I've seen in here before, but never been in. It is more or less the same as Mr Lee's cabin, if a bit messier. The cabinet is next to his cot, and its key dangles from the lock. I don't have much time, so I get straight to work. As in the depot, I am methodical and systematic; I work through the pile of papers in his cabinet, one by one. Most of it is related to the administration of Mizushima-00109, or instructions relating to different operations and machinery on the base. I would have loved to read more, but it is clearly not relevant, so I crack on.

Then I open the bottom drawer, and immediately know I've found what I'm looking for. A thin blue folder, no writing, anonymous, looking much more worn and ragged than the other pristine documents—which are clearly unread by Mr Reynolds. I remove it from the cabinet, and take out the contents.

Twenty, maybe twenty-five photographs. All women. I spread them out over Mr Reynolds' cot. A quick check of the folder shows that there is nothing else in there, no written document to go with the photographs. None of the women seem to be aware they are being photographed. Like the one Lily took, they are all looking elsewhere, engaged in an activity—sitting, walking, or talking to someone else. Mostly white, though a few are dark-skinned. Quite a lot with blonde hair, which I've never seen before, and is a lot more murky than the bright yellow I had imagined when reading about it.

I count them up, one by one. Twenty-four. Twenty-four women from Earth, that Mr Reynolds had brought with him to Hell. And none of them even knew it.

8

REFLECTIONS ON A MURDER

I AM SEATED on a bed of swag in the depot. My channel seems to have a fault, and there is a constant, low-level whine. There is a lot of work to do, but I am not working.

I am on strike.

Mr Ortiz came to my cabin to check I was going on shift, so I went, to avoid a fuss. But I am not sorting swag, I am cogitating on the circumstances of my sister's foul murder, and the possible motives of my chief suspects.

The Ays, the Ays... my problem with suspecting the Ays is that they lack both imagination and malice. They might have acted, if there was a danger of Lily stirring their sacred pot, but it would have to be a real threat to their status quo, and I simply don't buy that Lily's snooping was capable of that. On the other hand, I can picture it happening in a sudden flash of anger. And there is a lot of mystery surrounding the Ays. Ashton's glasses, for one—Lily must have taken them for a reason. Avery's death: I never thought of it as suspicious, but I do now. And their whole relationship with the six Bees—there's something fishy going on there, I just can't figure it out.

Then you have the Jays—or specifically, the Jay who had some sort of relationship with Lily. A crime passionel, as Mr Ortiz would have it. And you can't forget how divided the Jays were by Lily. She had managed to split them in a way I'd never seen before with a Family. Look at the Ays—they might have their bust-ups, but they're a tight, single-minded unit, really. The Bees have differences of opinion, but never in public.

In normal circumstances a Jay is cool, detached; I can't imagine one of them weighing up the costs and benefits, and deciding on balance it was best to kill Lily. But against a backdrop of dissent and rivalry (that I had been oblivious to at the time)... and suddenly, I'm not so sure. Sometimes I see a touch of Mr Ortiz in them—his cold intelligence, but also that capacity for a spiteful, petulant gesture if his pride is threatened.

The key, I've decided, has to be working out which Jay was having a relationship with Lily. The more I think about it, the more I realise I can take an educated guess as to which one was weeping at my sister's funeral. I can cross off Judas, who waylaid me in the airlock afterwards. And I'm 99% sure it wasn't Jeremy, who was bantering and flirting with me just two cycles after she died—altogether too casual to have been Lily's lover. Then you had Jupiter and Joseph—both on shift during Lily's funeral. They could have swapped with a brother, I suppose—but as supplementary evidence, a check on the Rota revealed that in the twenty cycles or so before the murder, Joseph had barely ever been on a shift with Lily. And Jupiter—I only have to remember him grunting from his bunk: *I said it was a mistake* and *they're dangerous*.

No, this is between Juan and Jolly—who, now I remember, were the pair in Banana, the cycle that Lily died. What was it one of them said? *I've seen your sister on several occasions recently, but not you.* So I've narrowed it down to a shortlist of two Jays. Now I just have to figure out which of them it is.

Meanwhile, Mr Reynolds has jumped up the suspect rankings after what might loosely be described as the photographs bombshell. I can't say *why* exactly, other than Lily clearly thought it worthwhile stealing one of the photographs. What I can't figure out is why a load of photographs from Earth is a big secret, or a threat to him. But something stinks. I may just be a pesky Ell, good for nothing but sorting swag, but I know fishy. And everything about that folder screamed 'fishy.'

I mean, all the women looking away, not aware they're being photographed? And the sheer volume—who needs twenty-four photographs of different women? I might not be au fait with Earth trends and habits, but I'm pretty sure this isn't normal.

When Jeremy let me out, I nearly told him what I had seen. But then, no, I figured: they've clearly had a good old rummage round his cabin themselves. They know all about the photographs. All of which means that Mr Lee was right—the Jays are in it for the Jays, and playing their own game. There must be loads of information about Lily and about Hell that they could have shared with me, but have chosen not to. Despite their fine words, they're only helping me out if it suits them. What was it Jeremy had said? *She might be a catalyst for further developments.*

And what does that mean, exactly? Presumably 'bait' would be a more accurate description. Maybe they suspect Mr Reynolds too, and want me to trigger the same reaction that—hypothetically—happened with Lily. Thanks, Jays!

In fact, I bumped into Mr Reynolds earlier, a few hours after sneaking out of his cabin. He was slumped on a sofa, in a grimy boiler suit. He looked weary. For the first time, I felt a measure of pity for the man. He had no Family either, and I knew he hated being on Hell. He glanced at me, eyes blank, and I saw he was a human, not just an Overseer; a human with all the same desires and motivations as other humans. I sat opposite him, and he raised an eyebrow. There was no point trying to interrogate him about the murder any further. I tried a different line of questioning:

"Mr Reynolds?" I said.

"Yeah."

"Can I ask you a question?"

"Shoot."

His voice sounded a bit slurred, my first thought was that he'd been on the pills. Made life easy for me.

"If you found out a big secret about someone, what would you do?"

"No secrets here," he mumbled. "Can't keep any secrets on a rock this size."

"Okay," I said. "But *hypothetically*, what do you think? Best to thrash things out in the open, or brush them under the carpet?"

He gave me a sudden sly look. "What you getting at? Eh?"

"I mean, let's say I found out Mr Lee had done something terrible in the past, what should I do?"

"Everyone's made mistakes," he said, slumping again. "But everyone deserves a second chance. Whatever you've found, I'd drop it, Ell."

"Leila."

"That's the one."

He closed his eyes, shutting off further conversation. I had to bite my lip to stop myself making some comment about the photographs.

I THINK BACK to seeing him in the airlock, the cycle after Lily's death. That awkwardness—was it just the reaction of an emotionally incapable man, unsure what to say to a grieving girl? Or the embarrassment at coming face to face with someone he'd just killed a few hours earlier? I need to speak to someone from Earth about the photographs, but the Overseers will protect their own— even Mr Lee, though he despises Mr Reynolds. I try to detach myself from what I think of them all on a personal level, and picture them, their hands round Lily's helmet, grappling with her. An Ay. A Bee. A Jay. Two Ays. Three Jays. Mr Reynolds. Mr Lee. Mr Ortiz. I replay the scene, time and time again, but I'm no closer to knowing which of them it was.

IN A COUPLE of hours, I'm going to be sharing a jeep back to base with Mr Reynolds, Jupiter, Aaron and Andy. The thought of sitting among my prime suspects, oblivious that they're all being weighed up as murderers, makes me giggle. I lean back on the bed of swag and sit up again immediately, as it bites into my shoulder blades.

I think and think—I feel like I'm on the verge of figuring something out here, but it's just out of reach. I'm aware that the clock is ticking: just 590 cycles, and then the killer escapes. Marple, what would you do now? The interrogations are complete, I've explored any suspicious circumstances, I've found some clues… usually at this point, she'd bluff the murderer into making a mistake, like trying to kill someone else. But how do I do that, without getting killed myself?

I brought Mr Lee's reader with me, so I take it out now. I find *Sleeping Murder*—written during World War

Two, kept in a vault until Christie's death, when it could be published posthumously as Marple's last case. I skim through the last few chapters—she didn't have any proof either, but she *knew*, because of something the killer had said; so she laid her trap accordingly.

I skip the epilogue of *Sleeping Murder* and bring up the first Marple novel, *Murder at the Vicarage*. Something about St. Mary Mead reminds me of Hell—a small, enclosed society; the stifling claustrophobia and social stratification; and all those secrets lying beneath the veneer of respectability.

It's a strange story in some ways—told from the perspective of the vicar, who couldn't stand the victim, and who looks on in a detached manner as Marple investigates. Nobody is sorry to see Colonel Protheroe dead, but justice must still be seen to be done. The vicar is so bogged down with the *how*—the clock that is fifteen minutes fast, the various exits and entrances to the vicarage, the sound of the gunshot—that the *why* is almost incidental. Griselda, the vicar's wife, reminds me of a Bee. I do this quite often with characters—thinking to myself *he sounds just like Mr Ortiz*, or *classic Ay behaviour*.

My attention is wandering, and I can't focus on *Vicarage*. My attention is caught by a big lump of swag, it looks almost too heavy to lift. It triggers a clear memory: an Ay holding some swag, threatening to throw it—we're outside somewhere, but I can't place exactly where. He's backing away, watching two Overseers, grey stripes down their suits, approaching him in a pincer movement. I'm standing with a couple of others—Bees, I think, though it's not clear. We're all watching and patched in to one channel, but it's just a wall of noise and shouts and crackling. I can see the fear in the Ay's eyes, darting side to side. He suddenly lurches forward and *hurls* the lump of ore at one of the Overseers, and there's a cry on the channel, but the Overseer ducks, the rock brushes off him and onto the ground. The other Overseer charges and the Ay grasps at him, clutching and stumbling, and the two of them tumble in slow motion to the ground. Then the vision fades away, the shouts still ringing in my ears.

What was that about? Which Ay was it, which Overseers? And why am I only remembering it now? I really, *really* hate it when this happens.

MR ORTIZ HAS informed us that there's going to be an Asteroid General Meeting next cycle, one of the tedious gatherings that take place every 100 cycles. It's been scrawled in thick black letters across the Rota. If the Overseers had their way, it would just be a chance for them to recite figures at us and try to motivate us—but occasionally it livens up when brothers and sisters start bickering with each other over some petty complaint. Lily and I, we would generally keep a low profile at the meetings—whenever I spoke, I could feel forty or so eyes directed on me, I could sense each one, as though there was a laser beam running from each eye to me. I'm not intimidated by any of them one-to-one, but when they're all together, my whole body just clams up and I can't speak.

I sit in the Community cabin, and survey the Rota. I could do without the Meeting now, if truth be told. Seeing all the Families there together—six Bees, six Jays and five Ays, while I sit on my tod, trying to look as though I'm perfectly happy by myself, picking my nails and looking out the window. Maybe a Jay will take pity on me and talk to me.

Inside, my headache has built to a crescendo. I can sense it pulsing—it feels as though my head is a giant glass ball—a single rash movement and it will shatter. I've got to figure out who killed my sister, and soon. I lean back on the sofa, and close my eyes. For some time I lie there, people coming in and out, minutes ticking by, a scream building inside my throat. These twenty people, sharing this rock with me, cycle after cycle. One of them the killer. This dam must burst.

9

ASTEROID GENERAL MEETING

Mr Ortiz: Right, everyone present? Ays?

Aaron: All here.

Mr Ortiz: Bees?

Brenda: Present.

Mr Ortiz: Jays?

Jolly: Yeah.

Mr Ortiz: Ells?

Leila: Er, Ell, singular?

Mr Ortiz: Right, of course. (*Pause*) Now, there's a couple of issues to discuss at this meeting. First off, Lily's death. Sorry, Leila, but it's got to be discussed, it affects the whole colony—and our productivity. Now, we're *not* here to discuss

the circumstances of her death, or the various
rumours—

Beatrice: Why not? Surely that's exactly the kind of
thing that should be discussed here?

Mr Ortiz: Because …

Beatrice: Why doesn't Leila tell us what she's learnt
from her investigations?

Jolly: Too right. It affects all of us.

Reynolds: They've got a point, pal. Better now than a
lot of bad feeling and suspicions.

Mr Ortiz: I'm not sure this is the right place for it.

Mr Lee: This is a forum for debate, not just for us to
give announcements and monologues. Let the girl
speak.

Mr Ortiz: Very well. Leila can share her fascinating
insights with us, *after* I've done my bit.

Leila: Hey, don't look at me. I didn't ask to speak.

Mr Ortiz: Anyway. What I wanted to say was—we've
got a real problem in the depots. It doesn't matter
how much swag we mine, if it's not sorted and
tested, it's not going to be collected.

Andy: We already have to waste our time doing some
Ell work.

Mr Ortiz: I realise that, but now we've got half the
manpower. We were using a system with two Ells,
now we've got to cope with just one.

Brenda: Meaning?

Mr Ortiz: Meaning we're going to have to seriously
adjust the Rota. I've discussed it with Mr Reynolds
and Mr Lee, and we've got a proposal for you.

Either one of each Family volunteers to do half their
shifts working with Leila in the depots—

Alistair: You expect one of us to waste half our time
down the depots? When we could be cutting ore?
Come on!

Mr Ortiz: Or, *or*, the work is split between everyone. It
would work out as roughly an extra shift each, every
fifteen cycles. But that won't be so efficient a system,
since everyone is doing the work sporadically instead
of getting into a routine—so we might have to
increase that to every ten cycles.

(Muttering, discussion)

Jeremy: I'll do it. I'll be our part-time Ell.

Mr Lee: Thank you, Jeremy.

Aaron: It's a waste of our strength, putting us on depot
duty—let the Jays do our shifts, they're good at that
kind of thing.

Mr Ortiz: Now, lads—

Aaron: And you know how our quotas have got more
difficult without Avery.

Mr Ortiz: Okay, we'll talk about it later. Bees?

Reynolds: What I want to know first is—we're talking
about everybody pitching in, but is *she* going to do
her share?

Leila: Me?

Reynolds: Yeah, you. I checked out the depot after your
shift. Still a complete mess—piles of swag dumped
everywhere.

Leila: Yeah, well. I'm on strike until I solve this murder.

Reynolds: On strike?

Mr Lee: Leila...

Mr Ortiz: Striking is an option for workers who are being paid: you're a sister, you've been bonded here, and you're not finished until we say you're finished!

Joseph: That's an interesting interpretation of your level of responsibility here.

Mr Lee: This is really not a helpful discussion...

Joseph: No, I'm interested to hear more. Is Mr Ortiz the arbiter of our productivity now?

Mr Ortiz: Don't piss me off, sunshine.

Barbara: Why doesn't Lily tell us if she's cracked the case? Then we can get on with finishing the job here.

Mr Lee: Yes, go on, Leila.

Leila: Well, if I have solved it, I'm not going to announce it here, am I? I mean, I've done all the interviewing and investigating—now I just need a bit of time to put it all together.

Reynolds: In your own time. I'm not having my girls working extra shifts in the depot 'cause you're too busy playing detective to pull your finger out.

Mr Lee: It'll be on her own time, won't it, Leila?

Leila: All right, all right! But it's not fair that—

Aaron: There is no 'fair' on Hell. We didn't like it when Avery died, but we've got to hold it together. There's less than six hundred cycles to go.

Ashton: For the community, Leila. We stand or fall together. You going around accusing people ain't going to end well.

Jeremy: It may not be a palatable fact, but one of us is a killer. I, for one, want to know who.

Mr Ortiz: There's no proof of that, it could have been an accident.

Judas: Accident!

Mr Lee: Can we agree that, provided Leila stops her strike and returns to shifts as usual, she is allowed to conduct her investigation as she pleases? Mr Ortiz?

Mr Ortiz: Fine.

Mr Lee: Mr Reynolds?

Reynolds: If she does the work, then yes.

Mr Lee: And if she comes to any conclusions, we'll hear them out respectfully and decide what action to take.

Mr Ortiz: I'm so glad that's all settled. Now, to get back to serious business. Extra Ell shifts: Jeremy will represent the Jays. The Bees…

Brenda: The Bees will split the shifts.

Mr Ortiz: The Bees will split the shifts. And the Ays…?

Aaron: The Ays will split the shifts too. It seems there is no other choice. But we're not fannying around with the tests and the acid. We'll shift the crates, sort them, and that's it.

Mr Ortiz: I'm sure that's fine. Leila, is that all to your satisfaction?

Leila: Super. I'm not holding anyone's hand, though. I know you all think my job's so easy, you can prove it now.

(Long pause)

Jupiter: So what next?

Reynolds: Well, the next item on the agenda isn't going to improve the mood much.

Brenda: Why? What's the next item?

Reynolds: Mr Ortiz?

Mr Ortiz: Yes, well. It ties in with what we were talking about at the start. Productivity. Fulfilling our quotas. Not good news, I'm afraid.

Ashton: Well?

Mr Ortiz: Mr Lee, do you want to...?

Mr Lee: Very well. A few cycles ago, the three of us finished a thorough inventory of the swag that's been mined and sorted. We haven't done one for more than a year—nearly half an orbit. The results were... disappointing.

Becci: We're under?

Mr Lee: Quite significantly, I'm afraid. If we had kept up our rate, we would be fine. We were just about on target when we checked last time. Part of that is down to losing Avery. More importantly, we believe it's down to where we've been digging. In the early cycles, we found the rich seams, and should have been getting *ahead* of our quota. Now, we're mining lesser quality areas, which means less swag. That's the big factor dragging us below quota, we think.

Andy: How far below?

Mr Ortiz: It's about 15% under at the moment. Without Lily, the rate's going to slow that little bit more. So to finish 15% under in five hundred and ninety cycles' time would be a good result—10% under would be amazing.

Ashton: But we've all been working to the bone! I don't understand how we can be under?

Mr Lee: In a way, it doesn't matter why. The most important thing is that we're not going to make quota when the Collection Ship gets here.

Reynolds: And unfortunately, Earth's not going to be happy. They're not going to say "There, there," and give us a chocolate biscuit.

Joseph: So what? What are you telling us?

Mr Lee: We hoped not to have to tell you this, that it would never be an issue. But Earth won't accept 15% under, even 10%. When we were first sent here, they told us they *might* accept 5% in special cases—and given that we never had a full Family of Ells, I think we could have made a case.

Beatrice: But what do you mean, they won't accept it? They've still got to take us to Earth, that's the deal.

Mr Lee: Actually, they don't *have* to do anything. The way it works—they'll drop off supplies and take what we've mined; they'll give us replacement brothers and sisters, Overseers—all starting their term early. But nobody will be permitted to board the Collection Ship. They return an Earth year later—about a thousand cycles—by which time we will have made up the shortfall.

(Hubbub, shouting)

Reynolds: All right, one at a time!

Aaron: You cannot be serious! You know how hard we've worked!

Joseph: And the quota is just an arbitrary figure *they* set—they've got no idea whether it's a realistic target or not!

Juan: So they're punishing us for falling short of their own arbitrary target!

Mr Ortiz: This may be true, but—

Brenda: We will not allow it. You promised. You *promised*.

Reynolds: Do you think *any* of us are happy about this? I want to go back to Earth as much as you do!

Mr Lee: Unfortunately, this isn't a situation where any of us have any choice. They will come here, the tally will be short, and what we've told you will come to pass.

Alistair: We won't let them. We'll—

Andrew: We'll fight this.

Andy: If we stand together.

Reynolds: Don't be daft. They'll have guns. You won't have a choice.

Bess: Don't underestimate us.

Mr Ortiz: And if, somehow, you overwhelm them, then what next? Will you fly the shuttle back to the Collection Ship? Will you fly the Collection Ship back to Earth?

(Silence)

Judas: They've got us over a barrel, the bastards.

Brenda: You should have told us. You're as bad as they are.

Reynolds: Come on, Brenda. We had no choice.

(Pause)

Aaron: Is it possible to make up the shortfall, if we push ourselves to the limit?

Mr Ortiz: In five hundred and ninety cycles? No. You might make it to 10%, but you're already working to full capacity. You'd just burn yourselves out.

Mr Lee: What we all need to do is be pragmatic about this. None of us has to like it. But the fact is, we're not going to be able to avoid another Earth year here.

Beatrice: It's not fair.

Mr Lee: It's business. None of this is happening for personal reasons. There's not some evil genius chuckling madly as he screws us all over. There's just a computer with some algorithms, examining the financial viability of Mizushima. It looks at the costs of the programme and the revenue brought in by the swag, and works out what the profit margin is. And, in five hundred and ninety cycles, it's going to tell the corporation who owns Mizushima, that we do not yet meet the profit margin that is required. *(Pause.)* Just business.

Joseph: Nice speech. Doesn't change the fact you should have told us from the start.

Mr Ortiz: We're not allowed to. Too much risk of it being demoralising.

Beatrice: Whereas now we're just peachy keen, are we?

Brenda: You Overseers. You like to think you're such big men. But you're here, alone on Hell, in charge, for nearly three orbits... and you don't even have the balls to say the right thing.

Reynolds: Brenda ...

Brenda: Don't. Just don't.

(Silence)

Mr Ortiz: So. Any other business?

10

CATALYST

LILY'S FAVOURITE BOILER suit (grey) is up to my waist, and I'm sat on my cot, trying to think of ways to make myself look more like my sister. I've swept my hair back in a way she liked to do. I've rolled around in her sheets, 'cause I once read in a book that smell was the most powerful of all the senses.

It's a classic gambit: dress up as a murder victim, and see if it provokes a reaction from the suspect.

I toy with the idea of smearing some ore dust over my cheeks, to give off a 'fresh-from-the-grave' vibe. But that's a bit... macabre.

"A bit much, yes, Lily?" I say aloud.

My plan is to try it out with Juan and Jolly. If I'm right,

and one of them was Lily's lover, then I might be able to provoke one of two results: an admission of guilt, or at the least an admission of being her lover.

Jolly is first—he's the only Jay on base at the moment, according to the Rota. I find him in the Leisure cabin, idly walking round the perimeter of the cabin by himself. Outside it's dark, and I'm distracted by the glare of the lights in the cabin. I walk towards him casually, meandering past tables and equipment.

"Leila." He nods at me warily, continuing to walk round.

"Jolly," I say, trying to load my voice with meaning.

"Not more questions?" he says. "I really can't tell you anything else, little sister."

"Don't worry," I say. "Just stretching my legs."

I follow ten steps behind him, keeping his pace as he circles the cabin. Inside, I'm disappointed. Not even a flicker from him. If he was Lily's lover, and had spent cycle after cycle in her company, he'd surely recognise the boiler suit, the hair. A Jay who wept at her funeral would be just as sure to break his stride when her ghost wandered in. He seems distracted, staring out the windows as he walks. After a couple of circuits, I give up and return to my cabin.

I HAVE TO wait five hours for Juan's return, so I strip off and take a nap on Lily's cot, getting into character. When I wake up, there's still a couple of hours to go, and I just lie there, my mind blank, staring up at the ceiling.

Eventually, I hear the bustle and clatter of a group returning from a shift. When it's died down, I make my way to the Jays' cabin, and find Juan on his cot, pulling off his boots, weariness in his eyes. I stand in the doorway, just staring at him. Maybe a ghost would do this. I don't know—but it feels a safer bet than hamming it up and drifting round the cabin, saying "Juan! Juan!" in a ghostly voice.

It doesn't matter. Juan's eyes meet mine, and he holds my gaze a fraction too long—and at that moment I know he was Lily's lover. No falling to his knees, no turning white with shock, but it was enough. For a second I had seen how he looked at Lily.

"You loved her, didn't you?" I say. "Lily?"

He looks at me dumbly. Stands up, reaches out a finger and thumb, and plucks at the fabric of the boiler suit. "Leila?" he says. "Are you wearing Lily's boiler suit? Seriously?"

"Come on Juan. I need to know. We need to talk."

"How do you Ells get so stubborn?" he asks, smiling. "You just won't let anything go, will you? Lily was the same. Tenacious little buggers."

"We prefer to think of it as being thorough. Finish what you start."

"Hey, it's an endearing trait in a way. Just a pain when you get on the wrong side."

"Anyway, stop stalling. You were sleeping with her, weren't you?"

He sighs. "Mmm. The only reason we kept it quiet was that there were only two Ells. Lots of times for us to meet while you were on shift. Occasionally our shifts clashed, but I was always able to swap with one of my brothers if I needed to."

"How did it start?" I ask.

"It never felt like we were starting—just carrying on where we left off. Jays and Ells—we're meant to be together, you know?"

"Yeah, yeah—spare me. When did this 'carrying on where you left off' commence, then?"

"More of a cynic than Lil, ain't you?"

"Your sheer wonderfulness clearly blunted her cynical edge."

"Hmm. Well, like I say, I always felt like there was something there between us—a tension in the air. Then one cycle—maybe sixty cycles ago—we were lifting some swag out the tunnels; we found ourselves pressed against each other as we dragged the stuff out. We had our hoods between us—I could only see her eyes... but, yeah, that's how it started. The trip back to base with a few Bees was the longest of my life. But as soon as we got back, we came straight here, to your cabin."

"Sixty cycles," I say. "How could I not have seen it?"

"You can't be cross with her for not telling you. She was only thinking of you."

"How so?"

"It was just the two of you... she didn't want you to feel like you were losing her. Wasn't the same for my Family. But she had to think of you."

"So they all knew, did they? All your brothers? Plus, Mr Ortiz guessed—and Earth knows who else."

Juan shrugs. "You can't blame me for telling my brothers."

"Good grief," I say. "And that's why Jeremy has been sniffing around. He saw the success you had with Lily, so he reckoned he had a chance with me."

"Don't be a drama queen, Leila," Juan says. "It's in our nature. Your nature too. It's like nickel, turning red with the acid. You can't fight it."

"You old romantic," I say. "I can see why she fell for your honeyed words. How did she like being compared to a lump of nickel?"

"I'm not going to bandy words with you. You asked me if I loved your sister. I gave you an answer."

"Earth! Touchy, aren't you? Just a bit of banter between an Ell and a Jay, it's in our nature, I thought?"

At the moment, the door opens and Jupiter enters. He stops in his tracks and stares at us.

"What's going on here, then?"

"It's Leila, brother," Juan says, giving him a warning look.

"I can see that, I'm not stupid. But something familiar about this scene, don't you think?"

NEITHER BROTHER MOVES. I look from one to the other. Juan is affecting a look of nonchalance, but I can see the tension in his bunched fingers.

"I'm just having a private conversation with Leila here. So why don't you be a good boy and fuck off?"

The word explodes like a firecracker. To publicly insult

your Family, to take sides with another, is a gross breach of etiquette.

Jupiter nods, gives a horribly phony smile. "We're not finished yet, brother." He walks out and slams the door behind him.

"So," Juan says after a short silence. "What are we going to do now?"

"What was that about?" I say.

"What are we going to do now?" he repeats pointedly. He sits down on his cot, looking drained.

"Okay," I say. "Well, I presume you want to find Lily's killer?"

"Of course I do."

"So let's pool what we know," I say. It's gratifying to be in control with a Jay. Normally they are one step ahead, teasing me, but this one is muted. That's what love does to you, I guess.

"Okay," I say, "Mr Reynolds. I take it you've seen the photos?"

"Of course. Lily talked me round into helping her break into his cabin. She told me about the photos afterwards, and I went in to have a look myself."

"What do you think?"

"Some of my brothers think there's a giant conspiracy, run by the Overseers—and it's all tied in to the photos. The theory is, Lily lets slip she's seen the photos, so they kill her to keep her mouth shut. You want my opinion? I don't trust the Overseers either, and something funny is going on, I agree with that. But I don't think it has anything to do with Lily's murder."

"Why not?"

"They're not fools—not Ortiz and Lee, anyway. If they needed to kill someone, they're savvy enough to make it look like an accident. And they'd have known Lily's death would just make the quotas more difficult. This would only be a desperate, last resort, and I don't see how Lily could have pushed them that far."

"So?"

"So this was an idiotic, hot-blooded murder. Guess who fits that description? We need to look at the Ays."

"And Lil had her eye on one Ay in particular, am I right?"

He glances at me sharply. "Yes, how did you know?"

"Ashton," I say. "I know Lily stole his glasses."

"You're right, she was suspicious of him for some reason. Wouldn't tell me why, but once she asked me to look at him—and see if I could tell the difference between him and his brothers."

"The difference?"

"Yeah. Which is ridiculous, isn't it? They're identical, so how can there be any difference?"

"Whatever it was—you're saying Ashton killed her because she figured this out?"

"It's my guess. I've got as close as I can to Ashton the last few cycles—shared shifts, struck up conversations, trying to figure him out."

"And you get anywhere?"

Juan kicks out at a spanner and it skitters across the floor to rest under a cot. "Nope. Ashton's a big, dumb oaf, just like the rest of them. No hidden depths."

"Seems to me," I say, "the answer is to focus on Ashton, study him together with his brothers, so we can figure out the difference between him and the other Ays."

"And then what? You might end up like Lily did. I say we bide our time and—"

"Ah, bugger biding our time. You Jays, you're big on talk, but sometimes you've just got to get on with it."

He glares at me, but I'm suddenly tired of the Jays and their smirking and games, and the sense that, for all their fabled sense of humour, they take themselves a mite too seriously.

"Tell you what," I say, "I'm going to deal with Ashton—you sit in your cot and bide your time."

It seems like a good exit line, so I pick myself up and make an exit.

I GO TO the Community cabin, but a check on the Rota tells me that Ashton is out on shift. Bess is there, and Mr Reynolds, who potters around for a bit, then leaves. I take a bottle of vitamin water, and sit down opposite Bess. She's chewing her fingernails and looking balefully at the floor. I feel a sudden pang of regret, that I'm not closer to the Bees, that we could have been friends all this time on Hell. I know Ells are introverts, and I've always had Lily and Mr Lee for company, but now my whole Family's gone, I realise how much I miss having a friend to talk to. The Jays are fine for flirting and joking, but I could never share any intimacies with them. And let's not even think about the Ays. But the

Bees... I should be sat with Bess now, the two of us consoling each other.

On an impulse, I go over, and sit down next to her. "You're still upset about the extra cycles on Hell, aren't you?" I say.

"Sort of. The extra time is annoying, but what really makes us cross is that the Overseers never told us. We can put up with the nonsense here—we tolerate it—but this was a *betrayal*."

"They're cowards," I say, though I don't really think Mr Lee is. "That's all it is. Too scared of doing or saying anything that might upset their precious corporation on Earth."

"Maybe they are," Bess says, and pats me absently on the knee. "Maybe. But what scares us, and we only realised this after the meeting, is this: how do we know that we're really under quota? None of us have a clue what the quota is, none of us saw how they did the inventory."

The idea is so novel and horrible that I can almost taste the bile rising in my stomach. I shift on the sofa uncomfortably. "But what benefit could there be for them to lie? Why would they do that?"

"I don't know. But I don't trust them any more."

My guilty secret is that I'm not *that* bothered by the thousand cycles that have been summarily dumped onto the end of our sentence. It takes off the pressure of finding Lily's murderer in time, and gives me a bit more breathing room. And not just that—I'm also sceptical that Earth really is the paradise that we've been promised. Respect, and a kind of filial love for the scientists that brought us to life, sure—but not the planet they live on. Based on the novels I've read, they've got the same problems and frustrations on Earth, just with more people. The Ays and Bees seem genuinely upset by the delay; as for the Jays, I think they're unsure like me. They'll argue about it with the Overseers, but only because they like arguing with the Overseers and causing a fuss. But I think Earth worries them. On Hell, they're cocks of the walk, strutting around—what will they be over there?

Anyway, I'm not going to admit my lack of concerns over the delay to Bess. "So," I say to her, "how do we find out? About the quotas and whether they're telling the truth?"

"We've been thinking—it's not easy. The only solution isn't very pleasant. We'd have to take an Overseer and force the truth out of them."

"What—torture?"

"Mmm." She nods. "But I'm not sure we're ready to go down that road, are you?"

"Once we do that, there's no turning back. It'd be out-and-out civil war. I mean, I know the Jays are getting pretty mutinous, but ..."

"Exactly. I don't think we could risk it. Not for the sake of a thousand cycles."

We are silent for a while, and stare out the windows.

"Listen, Bess," I say suddenly. "Imagine we're an orbit in the future—we've all left here, and travelled to Earth. Imagine if you bumped into one of the Overseers, like you're walking down one of the roads, and there's Mr

Ortiz, walking in the other direction. Would that be strange? What would you say?"

"I don't think I'd have anything to say to them," Bess says bluntly. "The minute we get off this rock, we're finished. I won't have to do what they say any more."

"I suppose. How about if you bump into me? We'll still talk, won't we?"

She gives me a flash of the Bee smile—mischievous, slightly crooked. "Of course we will, Leila. But remember, you'll be with all the other Ells when you get to Earth. You'll forget about us Bees pretty quickly."

I smile back, but I'm not so sure. Even if we don't share every secret together, the Bees are a fundamental part of my life—one of the cornerstones, along with the Ays, the Jays and the Overseers. Forgetting about them sounds crazy, as does walking past Mr Ortiz and ignoring him.

I remember something Mr Lee once told me—Hell would fit into Earth about 6,000,000 times. And that in a typical city the size of Hell, you would find 10,000,000 people. When numbers get that big, they become stupid. I mean, even the Community cabin feels pretty crowded when we have an Asteroid General Meeting there.

There's something about the idea of it that just sounds obscene—endless land and people, and land and people, and land and people. The more I think about it, the more I fancy a few more orbits on Hell, with my new sister Ells. Would it sound ungrateful to say I'd rather catch a later flight?

*　　*　　*

ON THE HANDFUL of occasions when someone attempts to murder Miss Marple because of her meddling, she is ready for them—often with a pleasant young policeman waiting to intervene. But I have nobody, and I am completely unprepared.

I am making my way to the depots in Tomato, just a solo trip to pick up some supplies for the base. My mind is on Juan and Jupiter, and my sister—who I had thought such an open book, and was keeping so many secrets from me. So I am paying little attention to the journey. The same landmarks flit past, the same constant bumps and tremors. In the distance, a shallow canyon comes into view, and I correct my course slightly. The plain slopes down towards the canyon, and that's when I notice the problem. I'm picking up speed, bouncing off the uneven surface—so I apply the brakes. But Tomato does not respond, the pedal just springs back. Again, I push the pedal to the floor but there is no pressure.

I start to panic.

The jeep continues to accelerate downhill, and I swear and bash the brake uselessly. I'm losing control, and bouncing around in my seat as Tomato lurches and staggers across Hell. The canyon is approaching fast, too narrow and too jagged for me to negotiate at this speed, and I turn sharply, pulling the jeep across the slope. I can hardly make out the rocks now, and there's a sudden jolt, as the jeep briefly leaves the ground. Time seems to slow down for a second, and I can feel every crack in my lips, every bead of sweat on my forehead. And at last I'm losing momentum, and for an instant I think I might just have pulled it off, but then from nowhere a ragged escarpment comes yawning up to meet me and there is nowhere left to turn.

I just about have time to manage to shout "*Eaaaaaarth!*"

And then I crash into the rocks, and the impact takes my breath away. The jeep rolls once, twice—I open my eyes and see the sky and jet-black landscape wheeling in front of me. Before I lose consciousness, the aimless thought pops into my head: *This is just like* Peril at End House, *I can't remember if she—*

WHEN I COME to, I am still strapped to my seat, and see that Tomato managed to land upright. Dusk has not yet come; I can't have been passed out long. It feels as though I've woken up from a snooze. Except for the crick in my neck, the bruises all over my upper torso, and the searing pain in my head, far worse than the usual headaches. I can sense crusty blood on my right temple, and it is infuriating not being able to itch it. I release myself from the strapping. I pad myself down, a vague need to check I am all there. All power has gone, the jeep is dead.

I open the door, gingerly drift down onto solid land. My legs are shaking, and I have to kneel. I want to pull my hood off and vomit, but somehow I hold it together. I count to ten, stand up, grab hold of the bonnet and pull myself over. I open the panel, find the brake fluid reservoir and check the levels—empty. There is a crack running along the bottom of the reservoir, and underneath is a murky stain on the bulkhead.

I give an angry hiss. If I had any doubts before that Lily was murdered, they've disappeared. Whatever she discovered got her killed, and I'm following her down the same path—hardly a surprise they tried to kill me too. Not the surest method, brake tampering, but far easier to carry out than my sister's murder: a quick check of the Rota, and two minutes' work with a chisel or screwdriver.

At least I know now I'm asking the right questions.

I find the flare in the back of the jeep, point it to the sky, and pull the trigger. I get back in the jeep, take a seat, and wait.

BANANA IS THE first to arrive. An Ay steps out, and patches through. "*Leila?*"

"Who is it?" I reply, suddenly terrified that it might be Ashton.

"*Alistair,*" he replies. "*What the heck is going on, Leila?*"

"I crashed. Someone tampered with the brakes, Alistair. I could have died."

He pauses, his breathing crackles. "*You all right?*"

"Shaken up; bit bruised. But I'll live."

"*Let's take a look,*" he says, and I climb out.

The two of us open the bonnet again, look at the brake fluid reservoir, and he dabs at the leaked fluid.

"*You're lucky,*" he says. "*Could have been nasty. But I'm not sure it was deliberate, Leila. These jeeps are pretty basic, they develop faults all the time.*"

I slam my glove on the side of Tomato. "Dammit, Alistair. Why is everyone so determined to believe these are all 'accidents'? Can you not just accept there's a killer here?"

"*Maybe you're right*," he says. "*I'm not going to argue about it. I know you must be pretty emotional right now.*"

I laugh, catch my breath. "Emotional!"

"*Anyway, there's not much we can do now. Do you want a lift to the depots? Then I can tow this back to base.*"

"You think I'm just going to *crack on* with some work? Are you insane? Someone just tried to kill me!"

He shrugs, looks around as though someone might rescue him from this awkward interaction. "*Take it easy*," he says. "*I thought you said you were all right.*"

And right there, I can see it: the reaction I'll get from the Overseers, from the other Families. Politely dismissive of the melodramatic and emotional Ell. After all, why would anyone want to kill *her?* Claiming someone sabotaged the brakes will serve no purpose, other than to alienate them further.

Play it cool, then. Don't let the killer know I'm rattled.

But be ready. Make the most of Jeremy as an ally: someone needs to keep an eye out for more attempts on my life. Because the most important thing now is to stay alive—whatever it takes to avenge Lily.

"Forget it," I say to Alistair. "I'm a little on edge right now. Jumping at shadows. Can you take me back to the base?"

Alistair fixes tow cables to Tomato, and at this point Cabbage turns up in response to the flare, driven by what looks like a Bee or a Jay. I let Alistair tell them what happened, and get into Banana, sulking. Thirty cycles ago, I would have chewed my left arm off for this kind of drama, but the reality of it is a lot more prosaic. I count my bruises and give up when I get into double figures. Being an amateur detective is seriously overrated.

11

EARTH

ANOTHER DAWN HURTLES past, another cycle. Predictably, the Overseers made a fuss about Tomato (more than they made about my injuries, that's for sure), but I placated them, and didn't stir the pot with my suspicions. What's needed now is a low profile. Let the killer think I've got all the questions out of my system.

Ashton has proved elusive—he went to sleep when he got back from his shift, and my next work shift starts before he gets up for his leisure shift. But I am playing the long game.

Not biding my time. There's a difference.

I'm avoiding the Jays. Jeremy has tried to talk to me on a couple of occasions, but I've fobbed him off. In a couple of cycles, he, and assorted Ays and Bees, will start accompanying me to the depots to learn the ropes. But for now, I'm cross with them—partly humiliated that they all knew about Juan and Lily and I didn't; partly annoyed that there's a load of information that they've been holding back from me—and not acting on it. If I'm going to solve this murder, I'll have to do it alone.

There has been a fault with the water purifier, and various Ays and Jays and Mr Ortiz have been in their element, marching in and out of the communal cabins, half-suited, with stern faces. Lots of hushed discussions and arguments about the back-up purifier, etcetera. They act like they are worried, but they live for this kind of mild drama, breaking up the tedium of the cycles. Nobody asks me my opinion, not that I would be any help.

So instead, I'm avoiding the fuss and taking refuge in Mr Lee's cabin. He seems distracted, but happy to chat intermittently while he examines some papers.

"How are you feeling about the recent announcement, Leila?" he asks. "You okay with it?"

I shrug. "I don't know. I mean, in a way—it'll be good to have those replacement Ells, won't it? I'm not that fussed about the delay, not like the others." A pause. "How about you, are you annoyed by it?"

"It is what it is. Obviously it's frustrating, but... it's nobody's fault. Raging and cursing won't change it." He stops fiddling with his papers and picks up the photograph of his family. "I just want to see my boys again."

Mr Lee doesn't talk about his pre-Hell life often, so I always listen closely to this kind of thing. "They were only kids when I left," he says. "They'll be grown up now. Young men." His voice is sad and empty.

"Why did you come here, Mr Lee? Didn't you want to watch them grow up?"

"Of course I did. Of course. But... sometimes, family life—Earth family life—is complicated. I made mistakes. If I could live it all again, I'd be with them now."

"What about Mr Reynolds and Mr Ortiz, do they have families?"

"No. No, I don't think so."

"They must be lonely."

"Family life's not for everyone. Look at the brothers and sisters here. I think an Ay or a Bee would struggle on their own, but you're coping very well. You've always been pretty self-sufficient."

"So what will it be like on Earth?" I ask him. "Will I live in a house with lots of other Ells? Or could I meet someone, have my own family like you do?"

"I... don't know, Leila. Don't forget, the whole programme was still in its infancy when I left. There hadn't been many returns at that point."

"Do you think I'll like Earth?" I say. Mr Lee is usually reluctant to talk much about Earth, so when he's in this kind of mood, you have to milk it.

"Like it? Well... you'll see things you never thought possible. Beautiful, breath-taking sights—I could try and describe them, but I wouldn't be doing them justice. On the other hand, you'll need to be careful."

"Of what?"

"People. People always let you down. Plenty of hucksters, crooks and human garbage on Earth. If they get a chance, they'll cheat you, lie to you, take advantage of you, screw you over, and manipulate you. Innocent brothers and sisters from the Asteroid Belt will be easy pickings for them. I'm sure there'll be safeguards in place, a system to manage your introduction to Earth life. There'll have to be. People will look after you and help you settle in—like you say, maybe you'll live with some other Ells. But just be on your guard."

I shiver. "I'm pretty trusting. That's my problem."

I look again at the photograph of his family. Two small boys and a smiling, dowdy woman. They look like warm, friendly people. Just like the twenty-four women in Mr Reynolds' cabin. I couldn't imagine any of them taking advantage of me or lying to me.

"So I've got a question," I say. "When they designed us, why didn't they make us… perfect? Nice?"

"I'm not sure I…"

"I know none of the families are *evil*, or nasty or anything. But we're all flawed, aren't we? The Ays, the Bees, the Jays, the Ells—we've all got personalities that can be difficult to work with. If they went to the trouble of shaping us, why not make us perfect?"

"Look, I'm no scientist. But I do know that the people who managed the whole process, they didn't fully understand what they were doing. They adjust and tweak, and try out various things, but they can't really know what a Family is going to be like, not until they're brought out the vats. No matter what they do, they can't stop the human spirit taking over. You can't create personality."

He returns to his papers, and I kick my heels for a while, drumming rhythms against his cot.

"Hey," I say. "Guess what I learned?"

"What?"

"Lily was sleeping with Juan. The last sixty cycles."

"Really?" He looks concerned. "Like I told you, it's to be expected, the attraction between Jays and Ells. But you need to be careful with the Jays. There is some truth in what Mr Ortiz said: back on Earth, the vast majority of murders of women were committed by their male partners."

Could Juan be responsible? I find it hard to square the emotion I read on his face with the coldness required to stand by while Lily asphyxiated. Unlike the Ays, I can't picture Juan losing his temper and lashing out at Lily. I guess what it boils down to is: how well do I really know the Jays?

"How do you think other people on Earth will treat us?" I ask Mr Lee. I'm aware I'm turning into a bore, pestering him with Earth-based questions, but none of us really have a clue what to expect. Even though we're in awe of the people that gave us our lives, it's a bit optimistic to think they're going be at all interested in us.

The Ays think it's just going to be a larger version of Hell, with more people, but I'm pretty sure it's going to be... awkward. Cagey. We're all complex creatures, and you can't just butt into a new planet and expect everything to carry on seamlessly.

It's like—if six Pees suddenly turned up on Hell, do we really believe we'd welcome them with open arms? *Hey, Paul, lovely to meet you! Let me introduce you to the gang!*

"What do you mean?" Mr Lee asks.

"I mean, are people going to be calling us by our brand numbers, and ordering us about, like Mr Reynolds does when he's in a cranky mood? Or will we kind of slip into society without anyone noticing? Will people even be able to tell we're *from* Families of brothers and sisters?"

Mr Lee says carefully: "The thing you have to remember about Earth, Leila—you'll have picked it up from your reading, I dare say—the thing is, we like turning everyone into tribes. It's how we all rub along. People stick with people of the same country, same religion, same colour, with the same amount of money. People who like the same music, the same books, the same clothes. We trust people who are like us. So... I'm not going to sugar the pill for you, Leila. I can say pretty safely that the Families aren't going to find it easy to integrate, not at first. It'll be tribal, all the way.

"Do I think Earth residents will start befriending brothers and sisters, even having children with them? No. Not yet. In a few generations, you might see change. But you, Leila—your allies will be the other Ells, and the other Families. The differences you have with the Ays and Bees will seem pretty trivial when you leave Mizushima."

* * *

BACK IN MY cabin, I think about his answer. It kind of makes sense. But it does beg the question—if we're going to be pariahs there, is it really going to be worth the trip, the millions of miles and thousands of cycles it will take to travel to Earth? It is beautiful there, by all accounts. The landscape—infinitely more lush and varied than the grey, jagged rocks of Hell. But let's not forget, that's from the perspective of people raised on Earth. And anyway, is that enough? Plus, a whole load of other questions spring to mind—like, what are we going to *do* there? More sorting and packing? 'Cause that's all I'm trained for. If there's one thing I've learnt from my reading, it's that you don't get something for nothing—there's no space for freeloaders.

So what will we do? Mr Lee doesn't know. Nobody knows.

I'M THINKING ABOUT the Jays, and what Mr Lee said about them, when that image comes back to me again. The bare leg, the burst packet of powdered milk. The malty smell. Only this time, the frame of the image widens out, and I can see it all. And it's me, I'm lying there in my cot in a messy sprawl of limbs and sheets, with a Jay. The packet of powdered milk is lying on the floor with some mugs, some powder spilling out under the cot. My long white fingers are stroking his chest, and the curly hairs that sprout there. But the surprises don't end there, as my gaze lazily stirs to one side, for I see a mirror image: an Ell (Lil! Even in this daydream my eyes start to prick) and a Jay, lying in the cot together, naked, dozing.

That's all I can see, though, no matter how many times my mind tries to rewind and see it again. So now I'm wondering, what was that? A fantasy? A forgotten dream? Or a memory, something that really happened, too early in our lives to recall?

Ugh. Was it Jeremy? Does he remember? When I get these pictures/memories/fantasies, my head aches even more than usual. I want to discuss this with someone from another Family, to see if they have them too, but who? The Jays, I just can't trust, and anyway, talking to them about us being in a sweaty tangle of limbs— well, that would just be gross. Something tells me the Bees wouldn't admit to it, even if they knew what I was talking about. And the Ays? Come on, I know they don't have daydreams and half-memories. Their imagination is like a giant empty house, bare of furniture, a clock ticking away in one corner.

12

LYING BASTARDS

THE NEXT CYCLE, I'm due to be at the base at the same time as Ashton and two other Ays—the perfect chance for me to take a closer look at them. That gives me a bit of time to pursue the Reynolds line of inquiry. So, during my shift at the depot, I pick up Reynolds' photograph from its hiding place and bring it back to base.

I find Brenda in the Bees' cabin—she's the Bee I trust the most, the one I think most likely to help me. We greet, and without any preamble, I show her the photograph Lily stole.

"What is it?" she asks.

I explain about Mr Reynolds' cabin, how I had a

look around, and found the twenty-four photographs. "Now, you don't need me to tell you something funny's going on," I tell her. "The Jays, they know too, but they can't—or won't—explain it. So I figured I'd come and show you—he's your Overseer, after all."

"Yes, he is."

"I mean, I thought this might have something to do with Lily's murder. Do you think?"

Brenda takes the photograph, examines it with a kind of frosty grandeur. In that moment she looks both scary and magnificent.

"Thank you, Leila," she says. "My sisters *will* be interested to hear about this." She gives a bitter laugh. "What a bastard."

"What?" I say. "What is it?"

"Leila, Leila. How many times have I told you? The Overseers know nothing. They're liars, frauds."

"I don't follow."

"What you've got to understand is—Reynolds is weak. Easy to manipulate. He told one of us the truth some time ago, when he was maudlin and homesick, and doped on pills. Which one of us he told, we can't remember. Perhaps it was me. But it was soon after our arrival on Hell. Ever since then, we've reminded each other, passed the truth back and forth, so it never gets lost."

"And the truth is...?" I said, wary suddenly.

"The Overseers aren't Overseers, Leila. They're prisoners."

"Prisoners?"

"We've all heard how Earth is suffering from overpopulation. But according to Reynolds, the worst overcrowding is in the prisons, which are bursting at the seams. Some—the worst criminals—are just waiting there for the state to kill them as punishment. Sometimes they're clogging up the prisons for orbits, the process takes such a long time."

I nod—I'd read about this plenty of times. "Some get hangings. Some get the electric chair. In some places, you get shot."

"Well, some bright spark came up with an idea to cope with the overcrowding. Rather than have them marking time, waiting for execution, cycle after cycle, they give them a choice: fast-tracked execution, or a trip to the Asteroid Belt, to do a job nobody else would take—to serve as an Overseer."

"No," I say.

"Seven Earth years, serving their time, as we serve ours. Then when it's over, a pardon and a return to Earth."

"He must have been lying," I say, but I've got that feeling creeping up the back of my spine, when you realise you've made a horrible mistake, that feeling of *Oh, bugger.*

"And for most of them... it's an easy choice. Off they go to the Asteroid Belt. Guaranteed death or a seven-year prison sentence on Hell? That's not really any kind of choice at all, is it? You cling to survival—it's human instinct."

"But how could they not have told us all?"

"And it makes sense, when you think about it," says Brenda, ignoring me. "How are you ever going to persuade a free man to go to the Asteroid Belt? Two years to get here, seven years as an Overseer, two years to get back. That's a quarter of your adult life gone, stranded in space, every comfort of Earth denied to you... and for what? Who's going to come to this *shithole*, Leila," and she's raising her voice now, and I'm getting alarmed, "except for a bunch of murderers, rapists and spies who have no other alternative?"

"So they're just here to keep an eye on us," I say, "keep us in check. And if they don't, they're buggered too. No way back home."

"Exactly," Brenda says grimly. "The bastards. The *lying* bastards."

"And the photographs?"

"As Reynolds told it, he accidentally killed a man in a fight, outside a bar on Earth. One stupid mistake, and the state decides to execute him. We never really doubted him; it was more the big lie that we were focussed on. But now I've seen these photographs... come on, Leila. What do you think he really was? A serial killer? A serial rapist? Somehow, he managed to keep the photographs as souvenirs. *Trophies*. All the women he killed, or raped—or both."

With a lurch, I think of Mr Lee. "And the others?" I say quietly. "The other Overseers?"

"Fedorchuk was already dead at this point, I think, we didn't talk about him. As for Ortiz, Reynolds said he'd boasted that he'd been in a gang, and killed nine men from rival gangs. Mr Lee—" She gives me a pitying smirk. "Your Mr Lee was a dark horse. Kept himself to himself. But a nasty piece of work, I'm afraid, if the state wanted to execute him."

"So, just so I've got this straight: we're sharing an asteroid with three killers-slash-criminals, and they're the ones in charge, holding the tasers?"

"That's about the sum of it."

"Earth! I thought it must be an Ay or a Jay who killed my sister. But it's got to be one of the Overseers, hasn't it? After all they've done, they're not going to have scruples about killing an Ell."

"You're probably right."

"Why did you never tell us, Brenda?"

"Why do you think the Overseers keep it quiet? There would be chaos if everyone found out. Anarchy! The Overseers would lose all their authority. The Bees are, always have been, a pragmatic Family. We've retained the information—collectively remembered it—but the ultimate goal is to finish our term, and get to Earth. Anarchy won't achieve that—can you imagine if the Ays found out, or worse, the Jays?"

"So why tell me now?"

"The photographs," Brenda says. "He's clearly far more of a scumbag than we thought. If he *did* kill Lily, you should know the truth. And don't forget the extra year. These bastards have lied to us and lied to us, and I'm sick and tired of it."

* * *

WELL, WELL, WELL. Just like that, Brenda has solved half a dozen minor mysteries for me. Like, the reason why the Overseers don't seem to have much knowledge or experience of what we're doing here. Certainly it seemed odd that they were the best-qualified men that Earth could find to run a mining colony in the Asteroid Belt. Also, the reason why they are so grudging about their presence here. As for Mr Lee... I don't really want to think about him right now. Maybe he was a criminal back on Earth—a murderer, even. Should that affect what I think of him now, after all the time we've spent together?

I talk with Brenda for a while longer, but there's not much left to say.

"What now?" I ask, and she shrugs.

"Whatever you do, you can't tell the Ays or Jays. This whole place is on a knife-edge as it is. The situation needs to be handled with... subtlety."

As I MAKE my way down the spine, the three names run through my head like a drumbeat.

Reynolds. Ortiz. Lee. Reynolds. Ortiz. Lee.

It has to be one of them. Jeremy was right—the Families have had their differences, but surely none of the Ays, Bees or Jays would kill a sister. The three Overseers, however, who I now know to be hardened criminals— it doesn't stretch the imagination to think they'd kill Lily, if they felt threatened by her. Brenda didn't seem to think any of her sisters had told Lily what she told me, but still… if she discovered the truth some other way, and was planning to tell everyone their secret, of course they'd silence her.

And Mr Reynolds has to be the chief suspect—the one whose photos had been stolen; a weak man, most likely to panic and lash out; and let's not forget, the man seen wandering around the tunnels, when he should have been with the Bees.

First of all, I have to confront Mr Lee. I can't keep quiet, like the Bees have managed. I have to know what he did, how he ended up here, or I'll go crazy thinking about it. If I'm to ever trust him again, I need the truth. So I suit up, commandeer Cabbage (highly irregular, but it's not needed for three hours, according to the Rota) and drive out to the depots. I drive slowly and check the brakes a dozen times. Stupid, of course—this trip wasn't scheduled on the Rota, and the killer would hardly try the same method again—but I can't really stop myself. Night has fallen. I hum to myself; I don't want silence right now. I rumble along the rough track, carved out by thousands of trips back and forth from the depot. Probably 95% of Hell has never been touched by our machines. And after we've bled it dry, for all we can get, it never will. We're just a blip in the eternity Mizushima-00109 has seen, circling the sun in its desultory orbit. Funny when you think of it like that.

When I get to the ore depot, Banana is parked near the airlock doors, at a perfect right angle. I enter the airlock, then go into the depot. Two Ays should be here too, and I can see one, industriously dragging crates of ore to the far side. Mr Lee is fifty feet away, on his knees as he unpacks a crate. Our eyes meet, and I patch him in.

"*Leila? What are you doing here?*"

"I know," I say. "I know what you really are. You're a criminal, aren't you? They gave you a choice of Hell or the chop, and you chose Hell."

He stands up. "*Who told you this?*"

"Doesn't matter. Just give me the truth. One: what did you do? And two: why didn't you tell me?"

"*Leila...*"

"This is your one chance to tell me. Now, or you'll regret it."

"*The second answer is obvious,*" he says, talking quickly and softly—no doubt listening for the tell-tale *click* if one of the Ays noticed us talking and patched in. "*We couldn't possibly function as a community if you knew our real background. We'd have no authority. You must realise that, Leila—you're a clever girl.*"

"All this time, though?"

"*We never lied. We just... omitted our true history. It was the only way to make these colonies work, you must see that?*"

"Okay. Go on. What did you do?"

The channel crackles with what could be a sigh or an exclamation. "*They called me a traitor. A spy. I didn't agree with what my government was doing. They were selling weapons to some really nasty people, responsible for tens of thousands of deaths. I stole a load of files, leaked them to the media, hoping if they got out in the public domain, they would stop it.*"

"And did they?"

"*God, no. They hushed it up. I got caught. Spent four years in prison while they interrogated me and put me on trial. I used to go weeks without any human contact. Four years in a tiny cell, allowed out for exercise one hour a day. Anyway… in the end, they gave me the death penalty. Then gave me this choice. They like to send the political prisoners out to the colonies. Can you imagine this place run by four Mr Reynoldses? God knows what would happen. Fedorchuk was a politico too, I think…*"
He trails off. There's a long, cavernous silence on the channel.

"Did Lil know all this?" I ask him. "Tell me honestly."

"*If she did know, she didn't tell me,*" he says. "*I swear, on my sons' lives.*"

I'm walking away now—an Ay has caught sight of me, and is watching us.

"*Leila,*" Mr Lee says, and I turn my channel off. Out the depot, straight into Cabbage, and then a wild dash through the darkness to the base. I arrive back, and hit the steering wheel with the heel of my palm three, four, five times. I don't know what I was expecting. He's still the same man I knew. But our relationship is diminished, somehow.

I add him to my long list of people I can't completely trust, which now stands at an impressive 100% of the residents of the asteroid. I don't want Mr Ortiz to find me loitering in Cabbage, so I leave the vehicle and de-suit in the airlock. Everything's moving too fast now, and I find myself in my cabin without being able to remember how

I got here. I have a splitting headache. I stew for a while, pacing from one end of the cabin to the other, turning on my heels every five paces. My mind is buzzing; I've got to do something. I make a trip to the Community cabin, passing Andrew in the spine.

I've looked at all the evidence now, I've uncovered the lies. I feel like I finally know: I've turned the kaleidoscope, and I can see who it was, their hands round Lily's helmet. I enter the cabin.

Inside, two Bees are eating a meal—Becci and Bess. I sidle up to them. "Have you spoken to Brenda?" I say.

They blink and frown. "Yes," Becci says, "she told us about the photographs."

"And now *you* know about the Overseers," says Bess. "A nasty shock for you, I suppose. But not that surprising when you think about it."

I take a deep breath. This is my Poirot-in-the-library moment. It's only to two Bees, not the whole asteroid, the murderer's not here to hear my accusation, and I'm not doing Poirot's shtick of accusing and acquitting each suspect in turn—but it's still my Poirot moment.

"Mr Reynolds is the killer," I say to them. "He had motive, he had opportunity. Lily saw the photographs, and somehow learned the truth about the Overseers' pasts. Reynolds trashed the depot, looking for the missing photo, but couldn't find it. He must have been terrified of the truth getting out, of how the Ays and Jays would react—and Lily threatened to expose him. So he arranged to meet her to explain, out at East 5. He goes missing for nearly an hour, with Andrew seeing him down by the tunnels, walking away from East 3. He meets Lily, kills her, returns to East 3, and—"

"And Banana?" says Becci softly. "What happens to the jeep that Lily drove to East 5?"

I falter. I hadn't thought of that. If I'd been able to keep my diorama up in my cabin, if the Jays didn't need their precious chess pieces, I would have spotted this.

"Huh," I say. "I guess someone might have given Lily a lift, then returned to base?"

The Bees adopt a politely attentive expression, but I'm aware it's a weak suggestion. Surely anyone giving Lily a lift would have come forward and said something by now. And now I think of it—sabotaging a jeep, it's not Reynolds' style, is it? If he wanted to silence me, he would have come blundering into my cabin and done it face-to-face.

At that point two Jays come through. The Rota suggests it's Judas and Joseph. Aaron follows them in, three paces behind. They have all just finished a shift, and look tired. They get drinks, collapse on seats.

"All right, girls?" Judas says.

"Oh, yes," Becci says. "Just been talking about the murder. Leila thinks Mr Reynolds is the killer."

Aaron glances up, as if noticing me for the first time. The Jays look at me with lop-sided grins.

"Good for you, Lei," Judas says, which I hate: only Lil can call me Lei. "Reckon you could be right."

Aaron stares at me thoughtfully, and rubs his chin with meaty hands. "How sure are you?" he asks.

"Well—" I begin, but Bess interjects.

"The thing is—it can't be Reynolds." And she explains about Banana to the others.

And then she surprises me.

"And there's a second reason it can't be him. I was there when he disappeared for an hour, around the time Lily was killed. It was Brenda and me there, up on the ridge. When he came back, he was pale. Badly rattled about something. And for a few cycles after that, you could tell something was wrong. He was too quiet."

Becci takes up the story. "So anyway, a few hours ago I was with him in his cabin. He was doped up on the pills—buzzing and fidgeting the whole time. And then he started getting really upset, and told me he'd seen Lily die, he saw who did it. I tried to get him to tell me more, but he wouldn't. He was badly scared, you could tell. I've never seen him scared before."

I stare at her. "He saw it? He saw who killed Lily?"

She nods. "That's what he said."

"Reynolds doesn't scare easily," says Joseph. "He's a fool, but no coward."

"I'll give him bloody scared, he should've told me," I say. "Where is he now?"

"He's sleeping in his cabin," Becci says.

"Well, let's go and wake him up!"

Bess puts a hand on my arm. "Leila, you're not going to force it out of him. If he doesn't want to tell you, he won't tell you. If we're going to find out what he saw, it will need finesse."

I can see her point, and don't argue it. If there's a guaranteed way of making Mr Reynolds clam up, it's for me to go storming into his cabin, demanding answers. There's a strained silence, broken only by Aaron in the rumbling voice of the Ays. "But I don't understand… what would Mr Reynolds be scared of?"

I hear my own voice reply. "We are one hundred per cent sure that we're alone on this asteroid, aren't we? Like, there's no way something else could be here with us?"

I must be thinking of Christie's classic, *And Then There Were None*, Philip Lombard and William Blore scouring the island, convinced a killer must be hiding out there. Bess gives a little half-giggle and the two Jays give me a funny look, like they're not sure if I'm serious or not.

Mr Reynolds. Overseer. Serial rapist. Prime suspect. And now, if the Bees are right, my best chance of finding out who really killed my sister.

13

THE EYES HAVE IT

I FOLLOW AARON up the spine, ten paces behind. In all the kerfuffle, I nearly forgot about Ashton, who should now be in his cabin, awake. Reynolds may be my chief line of enquiry, but I still want to get to the bottom of the Ays.

Aaron turns in surprise at the door when he realises I'm following him, and I give him my sweetest smile. He's holding the door, and I slip under his arm, to where the two other Ays are. Ashton, half-dressed, rubbing his jaw, stretching; Andy, cheeks puffed, doing push-ups. He stops and climbs slowly to his feet.

"Can we help you?" Aaron says.

Subtlety may be the solution to dealing with the Overseers, but it would be wasted on the Ays. "I'm conducting an experiment," I say. "Can you help me out?"

"What kind of experiment?"

"I want the three of you to line up in a row, and I want to see if you really are identical."

Andy glances at Aaron. "What do you mean? You know we're identical."

"Ah, but are you sure? You were identical when you first came to Hell, certainly—but after two and a half orbits of backbreaking work? How identical are you now?"

"Sounds weird to me."

"I used to notice differences between Lily and me. At first glance you're the same, but how many little changes do you think have happened to your bodies all this time?"

Ashton shrugs. "Seems like we'll get no peace unless we go along with it. You know how stubborn Ells are once they get something in their heads."

"That's the spirit, Ashton. Vests off, please, gents, I need to see those torsos of yours. And Aaron, can you take off your cap, so there's nothing distracting?"

The three Ays shuffle and line up by one of the cots. Aaron is closest to the door, then Ashton in the middle, then Andy. Though they won't admit it, they're clearly enjoying showing off, comparing bodies. I stand five feet away, hands clasped behind my back, studying the trio. There's a lot of sniggering and muttering, but I ignore it. I quite like this feeling of power, directing the three of them around.

There are cuts and bruises on their arms and chests, but I ignore them and try and focus on the bodies themselves. Up to the faces, the cut of the jaw, the position of the eyes, the ears, the nose. *What did you see, Lily?*

"Turn around," I say. "Three-sixty degrees."

They rotate slowly, jostling one another, Andy trying to push Ashton off balance. Ashton and Aaron look naked without their props—their glasses and cap—like I've never really seen them before. Their backs are the same, just like their fronts. I stop focussing and zoom out, taking in all three faces at the same time.

Aaron is starting to get restless. "Come on, Lily," he says.

"One minute," I say, and Ashton rolls his eyes, and in that one instant I see it.

It's the eyes.

Ashton's eyes are different, undeniably different to his brothers'. Shod of his glasses, standing side by side with his two brothers, you can see it. Aaron and Andy's eyes are smooth ovals, but Ashton's taper away like a teardrop. The eye sockets are shaped slightly differently too—I can't put my finger on how, but I'm right, this is a different pair of eyes. And it doesn't matter how long you live, or what kind of physical labour you do—your eyes don't change, they don't get warped by your environment.

Which means... which means Ashton is not a brother to the other Ays. Lily must have spotted this, when he took his glasses off for a shift.

I realise Aaron has wandered off to his cot, and Andy

and Ashton are putting their vests back on.

"The eyes," I say to them. "Ashton's eyes are different."

"What?" Ashton says.

"You're different to the other two," I tell him. "I'm sorry, but it's true."

"You really are pushing your luck," he says.

"Stand next to Andy—then Aaron can see. Aaron?"

"I'm finished playing games," Ashton says.

But Aaron has turned back, and is giving him a funny look. "No, let's see what she's talking about."

Ashton protests, but Andy sidles up to him, and he stands, sullen, while Aaron stares at them.

After a while, he grunts, and swaps places with Andy.

"Have you quite finished?" Ashton asks.

"Well?" I ask Aaron and Andy. "Do you see?"

Andy glances at Aaron. "Maybe. Maybe not. It's not immediately obvious."

"Come on," I say. "It is."

He wrinkles his nose, and his moustache moves up with it. "Do you know how the whole process works? To make us, I mean? Do you know for sure if there are or aren't small differences when batches of brothers are pulled out? 'Cause I certainly don't."

There's an ugly silence, as if someone just farted. Talking about the vats and the creation process is considered bad taste.

"It doesn't make sense," I say. "You know it doesn't. How can your eyes be different? I bet you Andrew and Alistair have eyes the same as you two. It's just him!"

Ashton stares daggers at me, and is about to speak, but

Andy cuts in. "Leila, suppose you're right, and he is... different, I'm not sure what your point is. We're still all Ays, pulling together on the asteroid. If you were right, it would make no *difference* to me. Aaron, would it make any difference to you?"

"Nope."

"Ashton, would it make any difference to you?"

He shakes his head, slowly.

"In which case, this whole thing is irrelevant. Certainly, it's nothing to do with what happened to your poor sister."

"But aren't you curious?" I nearly cry. "If Ashton is different, don't you want to know why?"

"Time for you to piss off, Leila," Ashton says, a frosty smile on his lips.

I stamp my foot and stalk out. As I leave, though, it may be my imagination, but I can't help feeling the atmosphere between the three of them has changed— strained and heavy.

IT DOESN'T TAKE long for Mr Ortiz to turn up. He enters my cabin an hour later, angry and less in control of himself than last time we crossed swords. I'm sitting on my cot, picking my nails.

"What's this I hear about you stirring up the Ays?" he says.

For all their bluster and alpha-male credentials, the Ays really are a bunch of pussies. Always running to Mr Ortiz if their nose is put out of joint in the slightest.

"Last I heard, the Ays were big enough and ugly enough to look after themselves," I say. (I read that in a book somewhere, a sassy heroine said it. Made me laugh.) "Why have they got you running around for them?"

He freezes, and I worry I've gone too far. Especially now I know he's killed nine men. "What did you say?"

"I asked you about the Ays last time," I say, "and you said you weren't their nanny. That I had to speak to them."

"That may be, but I'm stepping in now. This has gone on long enough. Now, more than ever, we need to be pulling together, not fighting. You're going to be working with the Ays in the depot!"

"I was just conducting an experiment. Is that so wrong?"

"You're in too deep," he says softly. "Back away, girlie."

"I'm right, aren't I? Ashton is different from the rest. His eyes—"

"Absolute rubbish. They're identical. Genetically, they are duplicates. As are the Bees, as are the Jays. How hard is this to understand?"

"But maybe he's from a different batch? A different vat? I don't know how it works—"

"You're right, you *don't* know. So drop it."

"I'm not sure why you're getting so cross."

He doesn't speak, but tenses his jaw, and I can tell he's wrestling with what to say. Eventually, he comes and sits next to me, pats me on the knee. My skin crawls. I try to swallow back a bit of bile.

"I'm going to give you some advice, Leila, for free. You'd end up learning it on Earth, anyway, but I'm going to tell you now. There are times in life when you have to learn to look the other way. To pretend you don't see what's in front of your eyes. Times when you have to do something distasteful, not because you want to, but because it's… what's it called… ah, yes—the lesser evil. And no matter how much you have to hold your nose, you do it anyway, because it's the only path left to you. The others get this: the Ays, the Bees, the Jays, they all know when to look away. But you Ells…" He gives a short, harsh laugh. "You've always had this stubborn streak. Now, I don't know if Ashton is different, I don't fucking care, to be frank—but regardless, it's only something that's going to cause a fuss. So we look the other way. And we get our term done, without killing each other. Yeah?"

No, I think, *because I'm Jane ruddy Marple, and you are a multiple murdering bastard, and I'm going to see my sister's killer pay, whoever it might be.*

I mutter something that could be affirmative or negative. He scowls and gets up, goes to the door. "This can be easy, or it can be hard, sweetheart. You want to go to Earth? Take my advice."

I've never responded well to bullies' threats. "I'm not one of your Ays," I say. "I'm not *desperate* to go to Earth. So don't try to threaten me."

"You think you're safe," he sneers, "hiding behind Mr Lee. But you watch your back."

I deliberately turn my back on him, and busy myself

with tidying my cot. "Don't worry about me. You just look after yourself. Lot of anger out there after your little announcement. I'd keep an eye on all those angry brothers and sisters."

There's no response, and I wonder if that was a misstep. Mr Ortiz seems in control most of the time, but he's liable to lash out if pushed too far.

Eventually, he just gives a low snort.

"Maybe. But something tells me it'll all blow over."

His footsteps echo out the cabin and I'm alone again.

I GO TO Mr Reynolds' cabin and rap on his door. I'm not sure what I'm going to ask him, though I know I can't push him about seeing Lily's murder, not yet anyway. As Bess said, it's going to need finesse to eke out the truth from him. I could always confront him about the photographs and the Overseers' dirty little secret, but let's face it, that would not end well. So I'll just have to wing it, and see what I can get out of him.

There's no response from within his cabin, which is odd as he should be awake by now. I give the door a shove, but it's locked. He must have gone to the Community cabins while I was having a frank exchange of views with Mr Ortiz. Irritating.

I've no interest in bandying words with Jays, so I go back to my cabin.

I'm going to beat Mr Ortiz, somehow. His biggest flaw is his arrogance; I just need to drive a wedge between him and the other two Overseers. And the best thing I've got going for me is that, for now, I'm the indispensable last Ell. Which gives me a grace period, for a while anyway, when I can do what I want. I can't play the long game like the Jays, though.

I do always have the nuclear option in reserve. I'd have to betray the Bees' trust, but it wouldn't be difficult to persuade the Jays of the truth of where the Overseers come from. Then, boom, stand back and watch. It could be the spark that triggers the Jays' revolution. (And leaves us stranded on Hell, with no means of ever leaving, let's not forget that.)

I have a shift in just under an hour, with Jeremy, showing him the ropes. I'm not really in the mood for it, but at least it will take my mind off things. I climb into Lily's cot, crawl under the sheets, and stare at the ceiling. I semi-close my eyes, and my vision turns into brown, rotating whirlpools, juddering anti-clockwise in time with the throbbing of my headache. I try to jump into the mind of my dead sister.

"Why didn't you confide in me, Lil?" I say. "Would have made things a heck of a lot easier."

I need to know if a) she was really in love with Juan, or playing him, for reasons of her own; b) if she knew the truth about the Overseers, and if any of the Overseers knew she knew; and c) what was so relevant about Ashton's teardrop eyes. As Andy said, *did* it make any difference? The truth is, I knew why Lily didn't confide in me—she was protecting me, like I would have done to her.

Mr Reynolds is the key, I remind myself, and I resolve

to ask Jeremy for advice on how to get him to reveal what he saw. Until then, there's nothing to be gained by agonising over it, so I clear my mind and watch the stars out the window.

I've read about people who find the starscape beautiful—but is it really, when it comes down to it? A load of balls of burning gas, all about as bright as each other, dotted around the galaxy—what's so beautiful about that? Whereas: look at a piece of quartz, the size of your knuckle—chipped off by the swinging pickaxe of an Ay. The random lines, the sparkling metal, the gorgeous grainy texture—there's beauty, right there. All over Hell, there's beauty, if you look for it. Inside the base, I grant you, it's an ugly affair, a mess of faded grey plastic. But outside, where the Overseers fear—it makes me want to rip off my suit and roll around in the rocks.

LATER, I AM in the depot with Jeremy, teaching him how to use the different acids on the swag. He listens carefully, follows instructions, and makes the occasional pleasantry. I told myself beforehand not to be charmed by him, that I can't trust the Jays; but when you're with someone in the flesh (or in the suit, anyway), it's a different story. When he's with his brothers, he's a bit more smart-mouthed, a bit more wisecracking; but on his own he's annoyingly charming. There's even a kind of old-world courtesy there (offering to help me with heavy crates, asking how my bruises are)—he can't have picked it up from books, some instinct must have taught him that Ells react well to it. Part of me wants to tell him about the brake fluid and my certainty it was deliberate sabotage, but I don't want him to get all macho and protective and spoil everything. Just having him watch my back is enough.

We are on our knees, sorting a new batch of swag into the different types, when I decide to broach the subject of Mr Reynolds. I tell him what Becci said—it will be relayed around the community soon enough by Aaron and the two Jays—and ask him what he thinks.

"You know what strikes me as odd?" Jeremy says. "Not that he saw it happen and didn't expose the killer. That's to be expected; the Overseers don't want the killer found, they want the fuss to die down. They want us to reach the quota without any drama. What I find strange is that she's saying he was scared. Mr Reynolds wouldn't admit to being scared by a brother or sister, not even to himself. Or scared by Mr Lee or Mr Ortiz, for that matter."

I stay quiet. Jeremy doesn't know that Mr Ortiz is a nine-times gangland murderer. But even so, it does jar with what we know of Mr Reynolds' personality.

"I don't think we'll be able to guess *why* he was scared," I say. "The only way is to get the truth out of him."

"Really, we need to get to him when he's been on the pills again," Jeremy says, stretching and standing. The pile of swag is still ominously big. "But we need the Bees on board. He trusts them. The only thing is—can we trust the Bees?"

"Remember your duplicate key, though," I say

excitedly. "How about I hide myself somewhere in the cabin beforehand? I'll hear everything when the Bees speak to him." It's a bit farcical, a bit sub-Wodehouse, but living through my own Miss Marple mystery has convinced me that real life can imitate fiction.

"It's risky," says Jeremy. "You make the slightest movement or noise, he'd hear you. And I don't think the Bees would go along with it."

"Why not?"

He scratches at his neck, even though he surely can't feel anything through the hood. "Well, what do you think the Bees get up to in that cabin with Mr Reynolds?"

"What? No!"

"I don't know for certain, but sometimes you just get a feeling."

"The Ays would never stand for it!"

"The Ays are oblivious to anything that's not shoved in front of their fat noses. If Mr Reynolds is careful, no reason why not."

I think of all the women in the photographs, all looking away from the camera.

"I guess I'll just ask the Bees, then—we'll have to trust them."

We work together for a while longer. Jeremy doesn't make mistakes, and I know I can trust him with the depot. All it takes is patience and an ability to follow a system, time and time again, without flourishes or showboating. I thought a Jay wouldn't be able to resist putting their own stamp on it, but he's followed what I've said to the letter.

I decide to ask him about Ashton too. I was planning to keep it to myself—the reaction from the Ays and Mr Ortiz rather dampened my enthusiasm—but Jeremy has been a good sounding board, and I want to get his opinion. So I tell him about my experiment, and how Ashton's eyes were different to his brothers. He listens patiently while sorting the swag.

"Peculiar," he says, when I've finished. "But without more information on the process by which we were made, there's not a lot more we can do about it. Is there?"

"I don't like it, Jeremy. Remember the glasses. That was a deliberate attempt to hide the difference in eyes: either by Ashton or by Mr Ortiz. Which means they've been lying. If it's a harmless difference they know nothing about, why the cover-up?"

"Perhaps. But, just because he's different to his brothers—what has he got away with? What crime has this genetic quirk allowed him to commit?"

"Maybe he's not an Ay at all," I suggest. "Maybe he's some kind of imposter. A good one—but he didn't count on the Ells spotting him!"

"Um," he says. "Maybe."

I don't think I've convinced him. He's failed to give me any good advice on the Ashton Question. Personally, I love the idea of Ashton being an imposter. If this were Christie, he'd be a cousin who emigrated to South Africa, come back in disguise to kill Lily and claim an inheritance.

But it's not Christie, worse luck, and there's no inheritance, no South Africa and no mysterious strangers.

We are stacking crates together when Jeremy stops and turns to me.

"Listen," he says. "I want to say something to you."

"Yeah?"

"You know what Juan and Lily had—I wondered whether…"

"Whether?"

"It could be something we had too. You know. Me and you."

I put my crate down and stare at him, through our two visors.

"Maybe," I say. "But first, I need to know I can trust you. If you start helping me, and not hiding things from me, I might consider it."

"Whatever you want."

"Answer me this first: what's the deal with Jupiter? Is there something going on between him and Juan? Did he hate Lily? Was he cross that Juan was sleeping with her?"

"How did you know about that?"

"Just answer the question."

He shakes his head slowly. "You've got it the wrong way round. Juan and Jupiter both wanted Lily. They fought over her, Joseph had to break them up. Bad business."

"What, so they were rivals for her affection?"

"I guess so. But Lily chose Juan."

"And what did the rest of your Family think?"

"What do you mean?"

"You were split, right? Camp Ell and Camp Not Ell?"

He shrugs. "We're not all the same, Leila. You know that. I'm like Juan. We think we should work with the Ells, that together we can beat the Overseers. Judas and Joseph think you come between us, cause trouble. Jupiter went over to their side after Lily's rejection; he became the bitterest of all. Jolly's on the fence."

I nod thoughtfully. I need to remember to treat the Jays as separate individuals, but it's difficult when I can't tell the difference between them.

"So?" Jeremy says. "What do you say? I've kept my side of the bargain."

"It's a good start," I say. "But talk is cheap. I still want to see evidence I can trust you."

He flashes me a wolfish grin. And for a second, I completely see how Lily fell for Juan, I feel it inside. The problem is, there's that other side to the Jays—you have their charm, but also their flashes of anger. Jeremy versus Jupiter, Juan versus Judas. And which Jay am I getting? Because I know Jupiter is lurking in Jeremy, as surely as Jeremy is lurking in Jupiter.

14

AN UNFORTUNATE ACCIDENT (2)

WHEN I GET back on base, it's to find another kerfuffle has erupted. Jeremy returns to his cabin, but I go to the Leisure cabin, where Mr Ortiz, Andrew and Alistair are talking in low, nervous tones.

"What's up?" I say.

Mr Ortiz gives me a cold look. "Have you seen Mr Reynolds? He didn't turn up for his shift, and we can't find him in any of the cabins."

"Hello," I say, "this sounds familiar."

"I'm afraid I don't find that very funny," Mr Ortiz says.

"Sorry to hear that. No, I haven't seen him. He was sleeping in his cabin when I left on shift with Jeremy."

Mr Ortiz and Alistair look at each other. "He's got to

be on the base," Alistair says. "There's only one jeep not in use, and it's still outside."

"Have you actually been in his cabin?" I say.

"It's locked."

"But he could still be asleep."

"Not for fourteen hours," Andrew rumbles. "And we knocked pretty hard."

"There is a master key," Mr Ortiz says, "but of course, of the four Overseer cabins, it would be in his."

There is a prolonged silence. Mr Ortiz breaks it. "I don't like this. We're going to break the door down. Come on, lads."

The three of them stalk out the Leisure cabin, the Ays wearing identical tight-lipped expressions. I follow them up the spine. I read once about a character 'dining out' out on a story, i.e. it was such a great anecdote that everyone in the city was desperate to have that person eating with them, lighting up their social occasions with this fabulous story.

Well, this is anecdotal gold, watching Mr Ortiz and the Ays go and break down Mr Reynolds' door, and every Bee and Jay on the base will want the pleasure of my company over a protein shake and a freeze-dried beef stew.

They reach the door. Mr Ortiz barks out, "We're breaking this door down, Sam! Shout if you're in there!"

'Sam'? Well, well. Didn't know that.

There's no answer, and Mr Ortiz moves aside for the two Ays, who are looking serious, although I know they just live for the chance to knock a door down with brute force. I suspect they're pleased to have me here as a witness, though they probably wish a Bee was here instead.

"Keep low," Mr Ortiz instructs them. "Lead with your shoulder." He carries on with some more tips about technique, gesturing with his hands, and I'm fairly sure the Ays are paying no attention to him.

Andrew goes first, charging like a bull, veins standing out on his neck. There's a dull *thud* as the door shudders. He steps aside stiffly, and Alistair takes a turn, brushing past his brother, but it's not enough of an angle and he hits it flat. He retires as well, rubbing his shoulder.

Andrew narrows his eyes, glares at the lock, and springs up into it—there's a *crack*, the door swings in, and he goes stumbling into the cabin. Mr Ortiz is next in, then Alistair, and I bring up the rear.

We all stop and stare at the scene that greets us. Mr Reynolds is lying on his cot, legs spread wide, arms against his body. He has some long johns on, but nothing on top, and I wince at the sight of his torso, mottled with liver spots, hairy, veiny. He's a big man, but there's not much flab there.

Then up to his neck, where a spike of swag is sticking out at a crazy angle. He's been skewered, and it makes me think of the Jays skewering the opposition king in their chess games. Dark red blood has pooled around his neck and into a circle on the sheets.

I want to be sick. I've only ever seen a few drops of blood from cuts, never this much.

His face is in a kind of rictus of comic surprise: not

scared, just a sort of look that says *what the heck?* It's a grim sight, but I can't bring myself to look away. Neither can the Ays, they're transfixed. Mr Ortiz is the first to react. He strides up, puts a cursory hand on his pulse—he's obviously dead, though—and then, with a sound that can only be described as *schlup*, he draws the spike out of Mr Reynolds' neck. A load more blood glugs out his neck, all over the sheets, and continues for a few seconds until there's a gurgle, then it stops. He holds the spike in his hand and faces us, splatters of blood now on his boiler suit. The spike is an evil thing, tapering to a vicious point—there's no way this was formed naturally: human hands worked at this to give it a razor-sharp edge.

Mr Ortiz looks cross. I mean, he looks really *cross*. "They want a war, I'll give them a fucking war," he says, more to himself than any of us.

Nobody says anything, waiting for Mr Ortiz to decide what happens next. Eventually he seems to come to a conclusion. "Stay here," he orders us, "I'm getting my taser."

He exits the cabin, and the three of us look back at Mr Reynolds. When Lily died, she just looked like a dead body, but Mr Reynolds looks exactly like a murder victim should. Alistair turns away and dry-retches, and his brother gives him a scornful look.

Mr Ortiz returns, holding his taser but not the spike, which is presumably locked away now. He looks at us evenly. "This is it, lads. It's the Jays, they're mounting a coup. And you need to decide what side you're on. Are you with me, or are you with the Jays?"

Alistair stirs. "We've no truck with coups. If this is the Jays, we're with you."

"Leila?"

But all I can think of is a terrified Mr Reynolds, witness to my sister's death. And Becci, announcing it to a cabin full of Ays and Jays, so that everyone on the base now knows what Mr Reynolds saw.

One of the central tenets of being a character in a Christie mystery: if you witness a murder, hightail it out of town or report it to the police (they never do, though). Because if you keep quiet about what you saw, or Earth forbid, try and blackmail the murderer, you will wind up as victim number two, as sure as night follows day.

Mr Reynolds, though, had nowhere to run to. And he *was* the police. *Exit* Reynolds.

"This isn't a coup," I say to Mr Ortiz impatiently. "This is all connected to Lily's murder. He saw it happen. The murderer killed him to stop him from—"

"Bollocks," Mr Ortiz interrupts. "Not everything on this asteroid is to do with your fucking sister dying."

"But ask Becci, she'll tell you—"

"Enough!" he shouts. "With us or against us, Leila?"

My cheeks are burning. I channel my inner Jay and play the long game. "With you."

"Good. So, here's the plan: first, we need to call everyone back, and find if they've moved against Mr Lee too."

He consults a piece of paper with a mini-Rota. "Ays— your three brothers are all working in East 8, with Jupiter and Juan. Mr Reynolds should have been with them all.

Joseph and Jolly are with Mr Lee and three Bees, setting up the South site. And Judas, Jeremy and the other Bees are here on base.

"Lads, we're going to confront Judas and Jeremy in their cabin. This much blood, it's got to show on the little fuckers somewhere. My money's on Judas, though I suppose Jupiter or Juan could have done it before going off on that shift." He turns to me again. "As for you, you can take Cabbage and go get the others. Go south first. If they've killed Mr Lee, go straight to East 8, tell the Ays it's war, and we need them on base."

"And if not?" I say.

"If not, just summon everyone back for an emergency meeting."

When Lily was murdered, Mr Ortiz was fuming at the disruption it caused the colony. Mr Reynolds gets himself killed, and it's all emergency meetings and civil wars.

Mr Ortiz is addressing the Ays, pumping them up, instructing them; I bet he's loving this, secretly. "After that, we secure the base," I hear him say. What does that even mean? Are they going to go and stop anyone from stealing the Rota?

"Let's go, lads," he says, ushering us out of the cabin.

"What about Mr Reynolds?" I point out. "You're not just going to leave him there, are you?"

"That's just a lump of fucking meat now, girlie. There'll be a time for burying our dead, but it's not now."

"But shouldn't we cover him or something?"

He shrugs. "Be my guest."

I approach the cot, but he's lying on the blood-soaked

sheets, and it's impossible to drag them out from under him. I stand over him, and look down at his startled expression. I'm never going to come into this cabin again. But I can't bear the thought of him lying there, staring out, while he rots in his cot. I lean over and close his eyelids. It's an improvement, anyway. Mr Ortiz gives me an impatient, long-suffering look, and all four of us leave the cabin.

I DRIVE CABBAGE down the southern plains, alone, in the dusk. The route is less clearly marked than the eastern route—not as many jeeps have passed this way in the last orbit. But I can still see my destination, the hills in the distance. I think of Mr Ortiz and the Ays, off to confront the Jays. I wonder if everyone's going to be alive when I get back, if it's all going to kick off with tasers and spikes.

I really don't think the Jays are staging a coup, and I really don't think they will have killed Mr Lee. I could believe they'll revolt one of these cycles, but... somehow this isn't their style.

I need a sleep. I should be sleeping now, according to the Rota. My last sleep was ruined because I couldn't stop thinking about the Overseers, and about Lily. My head aches. My head aches. My head aches.

I'VE NEVER BEEN to the South site, but when I arrive, I have the strangest sense of *déjà vu*. I spot Tomato, parked in the corner where the southern plains meet the hills. The Jays have repaired the damage to the jeep, and apart from a dent in the bodywork and a long scrape where it rolled, there's no sign of my accident. Out I jump, determined to get this over with, and get everyone back for the Emergency Meeting. I climb up a ridge to get the best view of where they might be. It's getting dark, and I have to squint to make out the shadows among the black rocks.

The atmosphere is ponderous; I feel like I'm dragging my legs up the slope. At the top, I stop and lie down to catch my breath. Then I survey the area for signs of life. The air is dusty, and I can't see as far as I thought I would. After maybe fifteen minutes, the cloud of dust clears, and I spy two figures, protected from the wind in an enclave. And a third, signalling to them about a hundred metres away. They're working with a theodolite; it must be the Bees. But for some reason I feel too shy to approach them, and tell them their Overseer is dead, that they all have to return to base. Where is Mr Lee?

"*Leila?*" The answer comes on my channel, but instinctively I know he's behind me. I spin round, and there he is, white stripe down his suit, thirty metres away on the ridge, walking my way. A Jay—Joseph or Jolly, presumably—climbs over the ridge and joins him.

"Mr Lee," I say, and patch in the Jay.

"*What are you doing here?*"

"There's been another accident," I say. "Mr Reynolds is dead."

"*You* what?"

"Someone stabbed him with a spike made out of swag. He's lying dead in his cabin."

Mr Lee mouths an expletive.

"Mr Ortiz sent me here," I continue. "I've got to summon everyone back to base for an Emergency Meeting."

"*Right. I…*" He sounds baffled, and I take command.

"Can you tell the Bees and take them back to base in Cabbage? And I'll go with the Jays to tell the other group in East 8."

"*Good idea.*" He approaches me with big, slow strides, and pats me on the shoulder. "*Good work, Leila.*"

He continues in the direction of the Bees, and I approach the Jay, who identifies himself as Jolly. This one's on the fence, I remind myself. Undecided what he thinks about the Ells. We clamber down the ridge in silence, then walk westwards for a while. Eventually, Jolly points out his brother, in a cavern a hundred metres away, on his knees and digging with some kind of oversized drill.

"Mr Ortiz is out for your blood," I tell him. "You and all your brothers."

Getting Mr Lee out the way to deal with the Bees was a cunning ruse. I'm not sure who to trust, Mr Lee or the Jays, but the Jays deserve to be forewarned about Mr Ortiz at the very least.

"*How so?*" Jolly says.

"He thinks that one of you killed Mr Reynolds, that this is a coup. It's not a coup, right?"

"*If it is, my brothers forgot to tell me.*"

"You'd better watch out, that's all I'm saying. Mr Ortiz

went off to confront Judas and Jeremy. The Ays were behind him one hundred per cent."

"*Stupid bloody idiots. What do they think is going to happen?*"

Joseph sees our approach and turns off the drill. Jolly patches him in and updates him. They talk for a bit, both Jays sounding worried.

"You know the best way to get Mr Ortiz and the Ays off your back?" I say, interrupting them.

"*What?*" says one of the Jays.

"Show him who the real killer is."

"*And remind me who that is again?*"

"It's whoever killed Lily! Mr Reynolds saw it happen, he was killed to keep his mouth shut."

"*But we don't know who killed Lily either,*" one of them points out.

"Well, you'd better help me crack the case then, hadn't you?"

JAYS LIKE DRIVING, and I let Joseph take the wheel as we cut across the hills to East 8. The journey is bumpy and unpleasant, and we don't speak; or at least, I don't. Who knows whether the Jays are patched in and strategizing together? But Jolly is looking straight ahead, and I can't see his lips moving.

I sure as heck don't trust them, but I'd rather be allied with them than Mr Ortiz and the Ays. And how about the Bees, which way will they turn? You'd expect them to follow the Ays, but at the same time they'd do anything to keep the peace and finish our term on Hell. They might be the key to stopping this from descending into civil war.

Joseph brings the jeep to a juddering halt, and we step out into the cleaner air of East 8. The Jays march off towards the caverns, and I follow. Soon we find Jupiter and Juan. The four brothers have a long conversation but do not patch me in, so I stand there like a lemon while they do their business. Then Juan disappears into the tunnels, and the four of us wait, shifting awkwardly, and the nerves become intolerable.

With their helmets on, I lose track of who is who. One of them is Jupiter, Juan's rival in love for Lily. What does he think of her now—did he grieve like Juan did? What does he think when he sees me?

I wonder whether his anger at Lily's rejection could have been enough to make him kill her. It seems too pat, too easy. But if Christie has taught me anything, it's that people kill for love or money, and it doesn't get much more complicated than that. Jeremy always said a Jay couldn't kill an Ell, but what if he's wrong? And if Juan and Jeremy found out their brother had killed her— we might just have to endure a war between the Jays, something only Mr Ortiz would welcome.

EVENTUALLY JUAN RETURNS, with Aaron, Ashton and Andy in tow, all covered in dust. There are too many people there for a proper conversation, so without any delay, the eight of us make our way to the jeeps. Back at the base, two of the Ays are confronting two of the Jays and examining their clothes for signs of Mr Reynolds' blood. Here, they are walking side by side, not exactly best friends but not enemies either.

At the jeeps, by unspoken agreement, the Jays all get into Banana with me, and the Ays get into Tomato. A Jay takes the wheel. I sit wedged between two other Jays in the back.

"So," I say, patching into their channels.

"*So,*" someone replies.

"Has anyone got a plan? This could all get messy. You haven't seen Mr Ortiz, he's really mad."

"*Leila,*" says a Jay, "*give us a bit of credit. You think we can't handle Ortiz and his five dumb bunnies?*"

The problem is, I want to say to them, no matter how cunning you are, it counts for nothing in the end. All that counts is who strikes first, and who strikes hardest. And that's why Lily ended up dead in a tunnel, choking on Hell's atmosphere.

But I'm forewarned, and ready to strike—just as soon as I've figured out which of these buggers is to blame.

15

ASTEROID EMERGENCY MEETING

Mr Ortiz: Let's call this to order, please! You all know
why we're here—

Joseph: *I* don't know. Why are we here, exactly?

Mr Ortiz: We're here because this is a state of
emergency, we've got a killer amongst us. Anyone
attacks an Overseer, it's an attack against all of us,
against the whole system—

Judas: Let's not be coy. You've accused us to our
faces. You think that one of the Jays killed Mr
Reynolds.

Mr Ortiz: I don't think, sunshine. I *know*.

Judas: On what grounds? You came to our cabin, with
your goons—

Andrew: Oi!

Judas: —looking for Mr Reynolds' blood, you found nothing. Where's the evidence?

Mr Ortiz: I don't need to see the skid marks to tell me when someone's taken a dump. This has got Jays written all over it.

Juan: And what about Lily? You think it's a coincidence that a dozen cycles after she's killed, and Mr Reynolds sees it happen, he's killed too?

Mr Ortiz: Oh, for fuck's sake, don't tell me Leila's got you started on this too.

Leila: Is it so hard to believe that the two deaths are connected? Are Ells so insignificant, would it pain you that much to consider—

Mr Ortiz: Yeah, well maybe they are related, maybe the first was a lover's tiff.

Juan: I swear, I'm going to…

Judas: For Earth's sake, none of us killed Lily. Do you really think a Jay could kill an Ell in that way?

Mr Ortiz: Ah—but you're not saying you couldn't kill Mr Reynolds.

Judas: I'm not genetically programmed to be attracted to Mr Reynolds, thank Earth. I suppose one of us *could* kill him—but we didn't.

Mr Lee: Hang one, hang on. Mr Ortiz—why are you saying they killed him exactly? Some sort of coup?

Mr Ortiz: Exactly. They want to seize control. They're trying to get rid of the Overseers, one by one. First they let Mr Fedorchuk die, when they could have cured him.

Jeremy: Oh! This gets better and better! Did we kill Avery too?

Mr Ortiz: Then they got rid of Mr Reynolds. You and I are next, chum.

Joseph: If we wanted to seize power, do you know what we'd do? Three simultaneous attacks, on the three of you. No warning. We wouldn't be stupid enough to put you on your guard.

Mr Ortiz: I'd like to see you try, you little piece of shit.

Mr Lee: Can I make a suggestion? We have to survive nearly a whole other orbit together, sharing this asteroid. We have to find a way to hold it all together.

Mr Ortiz: But we can't have people getting away with murder, either.

Mr Lee: True. Well, let's ask the rest of the community. Ays, what do you think about the murders?

Aaron: A Jay killing Mr Reynolds remains the most… plausible scenario. But there must be proof before we take any action.

Mr Lee: Bees?

Bess: We have no idea. But whoever it is—can they please stop it? If we fight each other, we'll never clear our quota, we'll never leave Earth, and what good will that be to any of us?

Mr Lee: Leila?

Leila: You know what I think. It's a classic double murder. Find Lily's killer, you find Mr Reynolds' killer.

Andy: And what's happened about that? Aren't you

supposed to be playing the policeman and figuring it out?

Leila: I have been, and I've discovered some interesting things. *Very* interesting things.

Jeremy: Do share.

Andy: No, please *don't*. The last thing we need is Leila stirring things up with her half-baked theories.

Mr Lee: We're straying off-topic. Mr Ortiz, do you agree that the community consensus is that we can't go punishing people on mere suspicion? The killer's been lucky twice, if he tries it again, he's sure to run out of luck.

Mr Ortiz: Last time I checked, we're the Overseers here. We don't need to *vote*.

Mr Lee: I'm not sure exactly what you're proposing we do with the Jays, though.

Joseph: What Mr Lee is too polite to say: are you planning to execute all six of us? And run the community with twelve brothers and sisters?

Mr Ortiz: If the alternative is you lot killing me, then yes, I am.

Mr Lee: I think Bess is talking the most sense—none of us knows who's doing this, but if any of us want to make it off Mizushima, the murders must stop now. Clear?

Jolly: Fine with us.

Mr Ortiz: That's all very well, but I want precautions in place.

Brenda: Precautions?

Mr Ortiz: Yeah. Everyone should always move around

in pairs from now on. No wandering around by yourself. And when you sleep, you take turns—there should always be someone on guard. We'll have to completely re-configure the Rota.

Leila: What about me?

Mr Ortiz: What about you?

Leila: Who's going to guard me when I sleep?

Mr Ortiz: The other families can take turns. And it'll be a hostage scenario—if Betty is on guard, and someone kills Leila on her watch, she's responsible, and one of Betty's sisters pays with her life. Same with me, same with Mr Lee. When we sleep, we'll have a guard outside our doors.

Jeremy: What? Seriously?

Mr Lee: Is this really—?

Mr Ortiz: It's the only way. Good incentive to stop these murders happening.

Jeremy: You expect us to take turns sitting outside your locked doors, six, seven hours? Are you that scared?

Judas: With a taser, let's not forget that. You're the only ones here with weapons.

Brenda: Mr Reynolds had a taser, didn't stop him getting stabbed in the neck.

Mr Ortiz: Exactly. And it's nothing to do with being scared, it's reasonable precautions. There's one of me, six of you, and excuse my French, but you're a devious bunch of fucks.

Joseph: Devious enough to walk through a locked door?

Mr Ortiz: As you well know, Mr Reynolds had a

skeleton key that fitted all the Overseers' doors. When you killed him—sorry, when *the killer* killed him—they took the skeleton key. So our locked doors are worse than useless.

Ashton: *Worse* than useless?

Mr Ortiz: Worse, because it gives the false impression of safety.

Mr Lee: Rather than go down this road, how about this—we have an amnesty.

Ashton: What's an amnesty?

Mr Lee: We leave a cabin open and empty for a few hours—Mr Fedorchuk's would be best. Mr Ortiz and I will both be out on shift. During that time, anyone is free to anonymously return the skeleton key to the cabin—along with the taser that went missing. If they *are* returned—no recriminations, no witch-hunt—things go back to normal for all of us in the community.

Leila: Except for Lily and Mr Reynolds.

Mr Lee: Of course. Except for them. But what's done is done. I'm trying to give us a chance to move on, to survive the next orbit.

Leila: What about justice? What about paying for your crimes?

Mr Lee: What about forgiveness?

Leila: It's not your place to forgive—it's *my* sister. And they're not even asking for forgiveness. Why don't you step forward now, whoever you are? Admit to killing Lily and Mr Reynolds, and we'll all forgive and forget.

(*Silence*)

Leila: Thought not.

Beatrice: But we can't carry on like this, Leila. Not with all the suspicion, all the arguments—

Aaron: And let's face it—the moment's passed. Maybe you could have caught the killer right after Lily died, but a dozen cycles later? It's too late, you're not going to find the answer now.

Leila: *Five Little Pigs*. Poirot solved that one *sixteen years* later.

Aaron: What?

Mr Lee: It's a book, on my reader… look, I don't think we're going about this the right way. The priority here is that we call a truce. In private, Leila may have her own opinions, as may Mr Ortiz, as may all of us. But for the sake of the community, I want a truce. And an amnesty for the key. Do you agree, Mr Ortiz?

Mr Ortiz: Fine.

Mr Lee: So, is there anything else we need to discuss at this emergency meeting?

Mr Ortiz: How about the Bees? They've got no Overseer now.

Bess: I'm sure we'll manage. The Jays have managed for orbits.

Mr Ortiz: Hardly a ringing endorsement. I'll help out. The Ays can get on with things pretty well without me.

Joseph: And what about the fact we've lost half of our Overseers? Are we going to be in trouble when the Collection Ship finally gets here? Or rather—are *you* going to be in trouble when the Collection Ship finally gets here?

Mr Ortiz: Don't you worry about Mr Lee and me. We'll be fine, thank you. I'll be giving them a full report of what went down on Mizushima during my watch.

Joseph: Well, that's super. We'll have our say too.

Judas: Hang on, though, brothers. This is important. When the Collection Ship gets here, it will be our word against his. And who do you think they're going to believe? An Overseer, or six Jays? He can say any rubbish he wants, and the Ays will back him up.

Andy: We'll only be telling the truth, little brothers.

Mr Ortiz: You've got that right. Like I told one of you punks, there'll be a day of reckoning, all right.

Judas: We want assurances, then. Someone needs to write down an account of what happened, and you can sign it. So there's no argument when the Collection Ship comes.

Mr Lee: Nobody's going to go telling tales, there's no need for writing anything down. Listen, this is the story we all stick to: Mr Fedorchuk had an accident, and died. Avery had an accident, and died. Lily had an accident, and died.

Becci: Mr Reynolds had an accident… and died?

Mr Lee: Good, you've got it. Mr Ortiz, are we in agreement?

(Silence)

Mr Ortiz: This stinks. But I can see I'm outnumbered.

Mr Lee: The bodies are all under the ground now. No one is going to disturb them. Anyone has any unfinished business, they can settle it back on Earth.

Joseph: Very well. And what about Mr Reynolds' cabin?

Mr Ortiz: What about it?

Joseph: What are we going to do with it? It may have escaped your notice, but space is at something of a premium for some of us. We can't just let a whole cabin go to waste.

Mr Ortiz: You must be kidding. If you think you can kill him, then a cycle later take over his cabin—

Joseph: So we're going to leave it empty, just on principle?

Beatrice: Come on, Joseph. Would you really want to sleep in there? All those sheets covered in blood?

Bess: Or is one of you Jays planning on scrubbing it out?

Mr Lee: I think it's best if Mr Reynolds' cabin stays out of bounds for the short-term, at least until the Collection Ship arrives, and we find out if more Overseers are joining us.

Leila: And how about Mr Reynolds? Is someone going to bury him?

Mr Lee: Yes—perhaps some of the Ays could arrange it?

Andrew: I'm not going in that cabin again.

Alistair: Me neither. I didn't mind burying my brother, or Lily—but I'm not cleaning up the mess of whichever sick bastard spiked Mr Reynolds.

Joseph: We're not doing it.

Beatrice: He's going to start to smell, though.

Mr Ortiz: Well, can I suggest that *someone* buries the fat fuck before he stinks out the whole fucking base? Otherwise, I'll dump him outside the airlock myself. Any more questions? No? Good—now, back to work!

16

PATIENCE

THE BASE IS still. No throbbing hum, no chatter. I pace up and down the spine, and for a moment I can believe I'm the only person left in Hell. That they've all gone, abandoned the asteroid, and got on board the Collection Ship. Leila all alone, with four corpses.

But I'm very much not alone. If it's quiet, it's a frosty, passive-aggressive sort of silence. Despite the grand talk of amnesties and truces, the peace that prevails in Mizushima is barely even surface-deep. Mr Ortiz and the Ays have colonised the Community cabin; the Jays have taken the Leisure cabin. Mr Lee is not seen outside his cabin, except to go on shift. The Bees are the only Family to move freely, neutrals passing messages between the two camps.

The Rota, meanwhile, is in a mess. The loss of Lily and Mr Reynolds, the attempts to provide cover for the depots, and the vague plans to make everyone stay in pairs, have caused havoc with the immaculate grid. Mr Ortiz has tried to adjust it, but it's all too much, with the pages covered in scrawls and arrows, and a holocaust of dots. It looks like the fevered scribbling of a madman. The Ays continue to go on shifts, taking their cue from Mr Ortiz, and the Bees seem to be going too. But the Jays and I, we go when we please, to stave off the boredom, always separate from the Ays and Mr Ortiz. Often, you'll see jeeps with just two brothers or sisters, or you'll get to the airlock and find there's no jeeps left. It's a shambles.

Our community has started to crumble. What is it that Yeats poem says? *The centre cannot hold.* I never understood that, but I feel like maybe I do now. I realise I haven't read anything on Mr Lee's reader for cycles and cycles. I've been so busy with my investigation. It must be the longest I've ever gone without reading, but strangely enough, I don't miss it, not when I've been dragged into my own private drama.

ASHTON STILL BOTHERS me. I sat facing him during the Emergency Meeting, and stared into his teardrop eyes. It's like a spy has come among us, an outsider, and there's nothing I can do about it. The Ays and Mr Ortiz prefer to close their eyes to the truth—I've no doubt the Bees would too. The Jays... I've considered telling the Jays, but it might break the fragile peace, and for what?

What can the Jays do about it?

So instead, they sit in the Leisure cabin, and play game after game of bloody chess. They've got more time on their hands now, so you might see two or three brothers facing the Holder of the Board at the same time, muttering and conferring. I neither know nor care who gets the board, when two or three of them beat the Holder. It is a deeply boring question I can't bring myself to ask. I wish Lily was here. Even Jeremy is less attentive than before, focussing on the chess and the seditious rumblings of his brothers.

I reach the top of the spine, and there is Mr Reynolds' cabin, still locked, and starting to smell. Nobody wants to touch the rancid body. Or at least, nobody sees why *they* should have to be the ones to cart his body outside and bury it. It's become an unsavoury battle of wills. Mr Ortiz, despite his big talk in the Emergency Meeting, has lost interest. I wonder if anyone will mourn Mr Reynolds, back on Earth?

It's a strange, coppery smell. Like the hydrochloric acid I use, but not so bitter. I swallow my bile and turn around.

Then I hear a soft scraping sound, coming from Mr Ortiz's cabin. I move closer, something rustles; somehow I know he's there, just the other side of the locked door, waiting. The two times I've seen him since the Meeting, he's had the look of a hunted man—heavy rings around his eyes, which were constantly darting around. He thinks he's next, and maybe he's right. No-one's tried to kill me lately, anyway, which is a plus.

Mr Lee's amnesty was a failure. He didn't say anything, but Joseph was hanging around when the two Overseers went to Mr Fedorchuk's cabin, and saw their thunderous expressions when they came out. Mr Lee needs to step up, give us some leadership, but we've had nothing from him.

Silence from Mr Ortiz's cabin. I think he's holding his breath, like I am. Slowly, I breathe out, turn around, and continue my pacing.

I PACE ONE final length of the spine. I've given her long enough to wake up. I turn off to the right, walk up the connecting tunnel and reach the Bees' cabin.

I knock on the door. Brenda answers, not groggy, but crisp: "Yes?"

"It's Leila here. Can I come in?"

Brenda opens the door and looks at me blandly. "Can I help you?"

"I just wanted to talk to you about Mr Reynolds," I say, squeezing under her arm where she's propped against the wall.

She shuts the door behind us. "Starting to smell a bit, isn't he?"

"Mmm. But I wanted to talk to you about his death."

"Still playing the detective, Leila?"

"See, I always thought he died because he saw Lily die. It all added up. Find Lily's killer, and you've found Mr Reynolds' killer. But what if it wasn't as straightforward as that? What if Mr Ortiz was right?"

"What indeed?"

"What's the best way to hide a murder?" I say. Brenda doesn't answer, but that's okay because it was a rhetorical flourish, I'm going to answer my own question. "You disguise it as the consequence of another murder. Lily's death didn't cause Mr Reynolds' death, did it, Brenda? But it certainly made it possible."

Brenda still says nothing.

"How long did you wait, Brenda? How long were you sharpening that spike, waiting for your moment? You couldn't possibly have killed him before: it would have ruined your precious chance of getting to Earth. They would never let you get away with killing an Overseer. So you waited... and waited... and waited. Must have needed extraordinary patience.

"And then Lily was murdered. And where I saw a tragedy, you saw... an opportunity. Am I right, Brenda?"

Silence still. Brenda watches me with a curious expression, head half-cocked to the side.

"And so you laid the groundwork, claiming Reynolds had wandered off for an hour when Lily died. Then Becci, the very cycle he was killed, peddling that rubbish about how he said he'd seen Lily die. Of course he hadn't seen anything. But she fed me the bait, so that afterwards I'd jump to the conclusions I did: that he was murdered before he could reveal Lily's killer.

"And meanwhile, maybe even at the same time as Becci is making her announcement to as many people as possible, you're in Mr Reynolds' cabin, stabbing him through the neck, letting him bleed to death like a porker in an abattoir. Then you lock the door, and off you go to work. And Mr Reynolds rots in his cabin until Mr Ortiz and the Ays break his door down."

Brenda smiles. "It's an interesting theory. And why would we kill our beloved Overseer?"

"I think he was raping you. Just like he did all those women back on Earth. Only this time, there was no police to catch him and put him in prison. He *was* the police. So you took it into your own hands. I don't know how long or how often he was doing it—"

"For as long as we can remember. In rotation."

There's a long silence.

"All six of you?"

"Yes. Always in a certain order. He was very strict about that. Usually it'd happen to each of us every few months, though it was getting more frequent."

"And the Ays never knew?"

She shrugs. "Why should they? It was always in his cabin, the door locked. And we never said anything. We couldn't. He always said, if I told anyone, he wouldn't hurt me, he'd hurt one of my sisters. I knew he was saying that to all six of us, of course, but still, you know? I couldn't be the one."

She's not crying—I've never seen a Bee cry—but her lip is definitely trembling, and she's fighting to stay in control. I stay quiet.

"And you're right—partly we were waiting for the right moment, but also we were just scared of him. He was strong, Leila. Violent. We knew we'd only get one chance."

"So all this time, you've been waiting for your moment, sharpening your spike."

"All this time, sharpening our spike," Brenda says, so tonelessly that for a second I wonder if that lip-tremor was a performance. "Must have taken more than an orbit. I can't remember. All six of us, taking turns in our cabin, rubbing and filing away. It's been ready to kill for the last few hundred cycles, but we kept going.

"And then our chance came. We were ready. We all played our parts. Becci spread the rumour. Bess and Betty went to his cabin on a pretext, and one hid the spike under his cot while the other distracted him. Barbara made him some food with pills ground up in it, so he was all sluggish. And then my turn. As I climbed on top of him, I reached under the cot, I pulled up the spike, and I stabbed him in the neck, Leila. Once, twice, three times."

She mimes stabbing, and gives a throaty laugh. "You should have seen his face. You really should. Good Earth, that was funny."

We can hear footsteps down the spine, and we both turn to listen, but they recede into the distance. "Of course," she says, "you've got no proof of this to show the Overseers. Or do you? How did you guess it was us?"

"In the Emergency Meeting," I say, "you talked about him being stabbed in the neck, and Beatrice mentioned all the blood on the sheets. But nobody had mentioned those details in the meeting. The two of you had gone straight from the South site to the room, and I didn't see you talking to Mr Ortiz or the Ays. You shouldn't have known about how he was killed, about the blood. Ergo you, or your sisters, killed Mr Reynolds."

"Ah. That was foolish. I should have kept my mouth shut."

It wasn't just that, though. It was Beatrice, feline, saying *there's weapons everywhere*; it was Jeremy and his insinuations about the Bees and Mr Reynolds; it was the photographs and what they meant. Those devious little Bees, they played me like a fool.

"But it's hardly proof," Brenda is saying. "And Leila, you must understand why we had to do it?"

"I understand. But I wish you hadn't used Lily's death like that."

"Lily wouldn't have minded. We're all victims here. You've got to fight back any way you can."

A pause. I realise how close we're standing, how tense my body is.

"So," Brenda says. "What now? You're not going to tell the Overseers and cause us a lot of grief, are you?"

What was it Mr Ortiz said? *There are times in life when you have to learn to look the other way.*

"The key," I say. "Give me the master key, and I'll forget all about it."

"The master key?" Brenda says.

"Don't play dumb. You took it, after you killed him. And I want it. I might not have proof, but you don't want the hassle of me going to the Overseers."

Silently, Brenda retreats to a cot and pulls out a key from under her mattress. "Quits?"

"Quits." I make to leave, but she calls me back.

"Leila."

"Yes?"

"The cycle your sister died—Mr Reynolds never left my or Bess's sight. We were together the whole time."

"So he definitely wasn't Lily's killer?"

"Definitely wasn't. It's Ortiz or Lee. Perhaps a Jay, though I doubt it."

And Ashton, I think. *Don't forget Ashton.*

I DON'T DARE investigate Mr Ortiz's cabin yet—I checked in the Community cabin, and he was there, occupying a table in sullen silence, while Andrew did press-ups in a corner. I sauntered up to the Rota, pretended to examine it, and left.

So, instead, here I am in the Leisure cabin, with Jupiter, Joseph and Jolly. They're engrossed in a chess game—the current Holder of the Board, Jupiter, against Joseph and Jolly. The pair are up a bishop but down a pawn, queens exchanged, and they're in the endgame now—Jupiter's king trapped in a corner, while the extra bishop allows his brothers to run riot.

My feelings towards Earth are starting to soften. It may be flawed, it may be even worse than here in some ways, but it's the only escape we've got. To stay on Hell is a form of cowardice. We've managed to hold the community together for the last few orbits, but now, it's started its inevitable collapse. I just have to make it out without being killed. And as long as there are people like Mr Lee on Earth, I should be all right. In all the books I've read, you have the good guys, and you have the villains. And the good guys will surely be on our side.

Nonetheless, it pays to be prepared, and at the moment, the Jays are the closest thing I have to allies.

"Jays," I say. "We need a plan for when we get to Earth."

"What do you mean?" Jupiter says.

"When we get to Earth," I say, "we're going to face opposition. Not everyone will accept us, will they? We'll be the minority, the freaks."

"Perhaps," says Jupiter. "But what's this 'we'?"

"Though it pains me to say it, Ells and Jays *are* meant to be together."

"A lot can change before we get to Earth, Leila," Joseph says. "And there's a lot of things we don't yet know. For now, we observe, and wait."

"You know, Lily had more balls than the lot of you," I say, suddenly angry. "At least she did more than talk and wait."

"We don't believe in acting without all the information in our hands," Joseph says slowly. "And that's why there are six Jays still standing, and why there will be six Jays at the bitter end."

"Easy, brother," says Jolly.

"And the Overseers? You don't trust them any more than I do. Never mind going to Earth, they might be killing us off, one by one. What are you going to do about them?"

Jupiter looks up from the chessboard. "Leila, you've

done plenty of good work here. Nobody doubts your commitment or your contribution. But there's just one of you left. It's time for you to sit back and let the Jays handle the Overseers. It's a question of how and when."

The brothers return to their chess. Joseph lifts his bishop, and with a jerky motion stabs it at Jupiter's knight, knocking it down. Jupiter snorts and takes the bishop with the rook that was protecting it.

"People are dying," I say to them, "and you think you're safe. Everything is falling apart, and you sit here and you play bloody *games!*"

I realise I'm standing, so I kick out at the chessboard. I miss, but a few of the taller pieces topple as I scrape the table. Jupiter cries out and Joseph uprights the pieces with a glare at me. Jolly puts out a hand to me, but I brush past him and exit, knowing that my cabin is the only place on Hell left to me.

WHILE MR ORTIZ continues to brood on the base, I go to the airlock and suit up. I step outside, ignore the jeep parked nearby, and head in a northerly direction. After a few minutes, I come to Lily's grave. This is what people do in books I've read—they visit graves and weep and reflect. I don't have any flowers, and there's no headstone or marker, just a pile of rocks.

I hate to think of her down there. Part of me is curious to know what she looks like now, what's happened to her body under the rocks of Hell. Whenever Lily got bruises and blemishes in the past, I would be half-disgusted, half-fascinated to see my mirror body damaged. It was like lending someone a piece of clothing and seeing it all ripped. And no doubt it was the same for Lily when I was the one with bruises. I remember when she got a big red bump on her forehead, and when I first noticed it, I put a hand to my own forehead reflexively—it seemed impossible that mine could still be smooth and pale.

I think about the Collection Ship, and how they might be bringing five more Ells with them. But I don't know if I'll like them, because they're not Lily, and they haven't lived through all this time on Hell together. They'll just be five new sisters, fresh out the vats, as innocent as I was when I first arrived. I want to warn them, to tell them the truth about the Overseers and Ashton. But how can I spoil their innocence; how can I send them down the path Lily took and the path I'm stuck on? We can be happy but living a lie, or we can know the truth and be miserable.

Or, very likely, dead.

I want to blame the Overseers, but I know it's pointless, even though they may have killed Lily and will probably kill me eventually. They have the tasers, they have the stripes on their suits, they have the authority; but they're nothing. Convicted criminals with less freedom than we have, forced to play a part and do what they're told.

All that matters is getting to Earth and starting again. And survival.

Because I promise myself this—I'll survive the trials of Hell, I'll not be killed, and when I've made my way to

Earth, I'll survive there, if only to spite them all. For the sake of Lily, for the sake of all those poor Bees, for the sake of Avery, and even for the sake of that stupid, dead rapist Mr Reynolds, I'll survive.

17

JIGSAW PIECES

IT'S NIGHT AND Mr Ortiz has left the base in Banana, with three Ays. I wait for half an hour, in case they have to come back for anything, then I decide it's time. Mr Lee is probably in his cabin, so I'm careful not to make too much noise. I take the skeleton key, insert it into Mr Ortiz's lock, and the door creaks open. His cabin is messier than when I last saw it—dirty mugs, clothes in small piles, spread in an oddly symmetrical pattern. In one corner, it looks like some small machine has been thrown at the wall, with shards of plastic and metal lying on the floor.

I wander round the cabin, in no particular hurry, but it's clear that the only things on display here are detritus or the necessities for day-to-day life on Hell. By his cot, Ortiz has dragged a canister of water and a crate of food bars and pouches. The information I want has to be locked up in the cabinet, next to the water canister. The key could be anywhere, but I suspect it's very well hidden—or that he always keeps it on his person. I hunt around for a while, checking under his cot, and at the bottom of the drawers where his clothes are piled, but nothing is there, just a stale odour.

I decide that I've come too far to stop now. A hammer is by the smashed machine, along with several other tools. I pick it up, and take a huge swing at the lock. The metal protests with a *scree* and a splinter of the lock mechanism pings out at me. I take another swing, and this time the lock gives way and the cabinet springs open. It contains several dozen plastic wallets piled neatly on top of one another, each one full of paperwork. No photos. The bottom shelf is empty, except for the Bees' spike, encrusted with Mr Reynolds' blood. I stand, transfixed by it for a moment, then get to work.

I pick up the first plastic wallet and leaf through it: an inventory of the Storage depot, similar to the one we use there. I put it at the bottom of the pile, and look at the next one. It consists of thousands and thousands of rows, each row having a metal and several numbers.

32. Aluminium, and then on the right a *17.4* scrawled by an Overseer's hand.

59. Nickel, followed by a zero.

At the top of the right-hand column, it says *Ore Yield*. This is a complete record of all the ore we've mined from Mizushima-00109—it's what they must use when figuring out how close we are to quota.

I plod on, through each folder, quickly getting a feel for which papers might be of interest, and which are just red tape. The paperwork has little to identify it—no headings, no elaboration of jargon. Often you can guess from the content what it's for, but other times, all I can see is a forest of figures or words I don't recognise. Sometimes, I see the Families mentioned—never by name, always by number. So there's a schematic of the base, for example, and each cabin lists its inhabitants—B1, B2, B3, B4, B5 and B6, all in the Bees' cabin.

But then, examining a folder which looks to be early drafts of the Rota, I come across one scrap, where the names have been scribbled out in full—not by Mr Ortiz, but by a hand I don't recognise. It's written at a skewed angle, with lots of spiky crossings-out, and deals with just the Ays. As I read down the names, I get a nasty shock: Aaron, Alan, Alex, Alistair, Andrew, Avery. Who the heck are Alan and Alex? And what has happened to Andy and—yes, Ashton? I take the scrap, and put it in my boiler suit.

I carry on, hunting for more juicy stuff. But there follows a glut of technical instructions, guides to the machinery the Jays operate, and I flick through them impatiently. Finally, I get to another interesting folder: a report on the Ays. Presumably, there's an equivalent on the Ells in Mr Lee's cabinet. I skim through the descriptions of the Ays' mildly differing personalities.

A4 has a stronger tendency than the others to lose his temper—handle him carefully.

A5 will fume for cycles over the mildest of reproofs—try not to criticize his work unless absolutely necessary.

It carries on in a similar vein for several pages. I put it back in the plastic wallet, and replace it in the cabinet. There are still dozens of folders to get through. My eyes are aching from all the reading. I blink three times, to beat back the waves of tiredness. A horrible headache has been needling away at the back of my skull, for Earth knows how long. I need a break, but this is the only chance I'm ever going to get to rifle through Mr Ortiz's cabinet like this. It's like his whole life has been laid out for me to inspect—neat rows of documents, an ordered, *predictable* life—nothing like the mess in Mr Reynolds' cabinet (who I suspect had destroyed the majority of his documents).

So I get back to my work, I shuffle through the pages, and with painstaking care I examine everything he has. I pick up some useful information, some oddities, dozens of jigsaw pieces that slowly fit together. When I'm finished, I look at the clock and realise I've been here for five hours. Mr Ortiz is due back on base in just over an hour. I make a vague attempt to tidy the cabinet, but it's pointless, since Mr Ortiz will see the lock is broken as soon as he goes to open it. I close the cabinet door—then as an afterthought, I open it, withdraw the Bees' spike and wrap it in a sheet. Then

I close it again, take the hammer, and tap at the flimsy lock to push it back into place, so that it won't appear broken at first glance. Finally, I take some wire cutters and snip the wires behind the cupboard, so that his lights don't work. It is night, and it will buy me a bit more time before the next cycle begins, and he notices the broken lock.

When I get back to my cabin, I find a Jay snooping around.

"Oi," I say, "Jeremy?"

"I am he."

"What are you up to?"

"Never mind me, where have you been, little Leila? You weren't with Mr Lee. I checked."

"I'm sorry, are you my Overseer? No? Then it's none of your business."

"All right, all right. Just keeping an eye out for you. Dangerous times, Leila. All of us looking over our shoulders."

I slip the spike-in-a-sheet under my cot, but Jeremy notices it. "What's that, then?"

"Jeremy, do I have to kick you out of my cabin, or will you respect my privacy?"

"Privacy! In this place! You're on the wrong asteroid if you want some of that, my girl."

"Don't *my girl* me."

He grins, lurches forward and kisses me hard on the lips. I respond at first, then push him back, and wipe his saliva off my lips.

"Don't be a fool, Jeremy."

He's still grinning. "This feels right. Don't tell me you don't think the same."

"All I know is, there's a killer on the loose, we're on the brink of civil war, all kinds of funny business are going on—this is *not* the time for sordid liaisons."

"That's not what Lily and Juan thought."

"Yeah, well."

"Suit yourself. So what *have* you found out, Leila? What's the big secret?"

I don't respond. "I'm right, aren't I?" he says. "You've found something out! Come on, tell brother Jeremy."

"No."

"Come on, you need the help."

"You're all sweetness and light now, but when you Jays get together, I don't know which way you'd turn." A sudden thought hits me. "Were you *sent* here? To try and seduce me, winkle out what I've learned?"

"Leila! No, I came to check up on you." He looks hurt. "Have it your way, then. I don't want to know your poxy secrets."

"Are you even Jeremy? You could be posing as him."

"Of course I'm bloody Jeremy."

"Show me your brand, then."

His lip curls. "Jays don't show their brands to anyone."

"Jeremy would show it to me, if I asked."

He stares at me for a few seconds. Then, with a wrench, he pulls the band of his trousers down, to show the brand on his right hip. It's not easy to make out on his black, pock-marked skin, and the number is faded and smudged, but it is, indubitably, a 5.

"Happy?" he says.

"Don't be like that. Listen, I'll tell you this much: if anything should happen to me"—I've always wanted to say that—"all the answers can be found in Mr Ortiz's cabinet. Get to that, by any means necessary, and you will figure it out."

"Okay," says Jeremy, frowning. "So Mr Ortiz is the killer?"

"Just look in the cabinet. And forget about Mr Reynolds. His death is nothing to do with this."

"You're not going to do anything dangerous, are you?"

"I can look after myself."

"That's what Lily thought."

It's a low blow, but I guess he has a point. I sit down on my cot, suddenly exhausted, and he flops down beside me, leaning back against the pillow. I lean back too, and rest my head on his belly.

"So…" he says.

"Shut up," I reply, staring up at the ceiling. "This is nice."

We lie like that for some time, and I drift in and out of sleep.

I DREAM OF being in a glass box, while silent, faceless men poke at me and scribble on their clipboards. I dream of an eternity in a cabin even smaller than this one, the stars creeping past the pothole window, my voice raw and broken because I've spent so long screaming. I dream of the depot, the bloody depot, the rows and rows of crates, walking and walking down the same rows and rows of crates, until I realise I've been walking for an hour; and I've started to recognise some of the crates, even though they're all virtually indistinguishable, and somehow I've been walking round in a giant circle.

I WAKE UP, feverish and with a pain at my temples. At some point, Jeremy slipped out from under me—something I dimly realised at the time, during my half-dreaming. I'm alone now.

My eyes snap open, and I scrabble under the cot. But the spike's still there. I take the sheet off and lift it, doing my best not to look at the crusted blood of Mr Reynolds. I try and imagine myself stabbing someone with it, the way I saw Brenda demonstrating. My fingers clench and unclench as I try to get purchase on the spike. Two pillows are lying among all the junk at the opposite end of the cabin. I cover the ground in four steps, and jab at the pillows with the spike, ripping through the fabric as smoothly as if it is water.

I withdraw it, slowly. That wasn't so hard. But now I try to imagine there's a human face on the pillows, yelling, pleading; I think of the blood, gushing out, spraying the cot and me. I think of the sound the spike made when Mr Ortiz withdrew it from Mr Reynolds, that soft *schlup*. I wonder what sound it makes when it plunges in.

I'm not so sure I've got the will to do it, when you think like that. Brenda is a cold fish indeed. I remember her in the Emergency Meeting, hours after killing her

Overseer, asking questions in a concerned voice and tutting about the clean-up operation. Nerves of steel, our Brenda.

My eyes are sticky with sleep, and the taste of spoilt food fills my mouth. I do some stretches, and try to drag myself to an alert state. Time has always been on my side—a bit too much bloody time, if I'm honest—but now it's slipping through my fingers. Sunrise is not for another hour, and Mr Ortiz should—*should*—be asleep after a long shift. I raise the spike again, pass it from left hand to right, to left, to right. I point the tip at Lily's cot, and utter a silent prayer to her—wherever she might be, whether stuck in those bones under the surface of Hell or in a better place. I think of Macbeth, agonizing over killing King Duncan: *If it were done when 'tis done, then 'twere well it were done quickly*. I didn't read much Shakespeare, too many words I didn't understand, too much that didn't make sense. But I understood that now, all right.

I march out my cabin, spike gripped in my right hand, skeleton key in my left. The spine is empty, which is just as well. I'm not too worried about a Jay or a Bee seeing me—they know when to look the other way. But the Ays mustn't see me, they would derail my whole plan. I stride past their tunnel without incident, and carry on up to Mr Ortiz's tunnel. I slow down as I approach his door.

This time, there is no heavy breathing on the other side. I can hear a gentle snoring, though: half-snort, then a low whistle. Half-snort, then a low whistle.

I listen to the rhythm for a full minute. Lily's spirit is

with me at this moment, and the cold fury of the Bees. I readjust my grip on the spike, and insert the skeleton key into the lock.

18

MEMORY LANE

"Ortiz. Wake up, Ortiz."

He grunts, and then one eye flicks open. He starts, and makes to jump up, but stops when I press the spike against his throat.

"What the fuck?"

I'm straddling him, my weight pressing down on his chest, my knees blocking his arms. My arm is holding the spike, an occasional tremble, but I've got it under control. In the semi-darkness, I can hardly make out his expression, but I think he's afraid.

"Hello, Mr Ortiz. You're thinking to yourself, can I throw her off? And the answer is, yes, you *could*, but by the time you have, this spike will have cut your throat."

"You?" he says. "You killed Sam? Your own sister, too?"

"Nope," I reply. "I'm just using the killer's *modus operandi*. But we'll get to that. First of all, I've got some questions for you."

"I don't know what the *fuck*—"

He gives a startled squeal as I press the spike into his windpipe.

"Listen, numbnuts," I say. "The first thing you've got to remember is, you're not the boss any more. In here, at this moment, you're the bitch and I'm the Overseer. Yes?"

"Yes," he wheezes, after a pause.

"Now," I say, "I've spent some time looking through your cabinet. So I've been putting all the pieces together. I don't have the whole picture, I don't know all the answers, but... I've got a pretty good idea. So. Here's what we're going to do. I'm going to ask you some questions. You're going to answer them truthfully, as best you can. If I think you're lying to me, I slit your throat."

"I—"

"No, no," I shush him. "Leila's talking at the moment. Now, just to warn you, I'm not an idiot, Ortiz. I may slip you some questions where I *know* the answer, to check that you're telling me the truth. Sneaky, hmm? So those are the ground rules. Everything clear?"

"Yeah."

"No second chances. One lie, and I cut, and get the answers from Mr Lee instead. In fact, to avoid unpleasantness, can we pretend we've done the whole silly thing where you test me and tell me a little lie, and I draw blood to show you that I'm not bluffing? Can we skip that whole charade? Let's pretend it's already happened: you've called my bluff, I've shown you I'm serious, now we can get down to real business."

"Get on with it, you crazy bitch."

"I'll pretend I didn't hear that."

"Go on. Ask me your stupid questions. But for the last bloody time, I do not know who killed your sister."

"We'll come to that. But first, question number one: how old am I?"

His eyes widen.

"Or, to put it a way you can answer, how long have we been on this asteroid?"

There's a short silence. "You know how long, Leila," he says carefully, eyeing the spike.

"Don't say six Earth years, Ortiz," I say. "Don't say two orbits. Remember what I said about lies."

"I... can't. They'll kill me. Or worse, leave me here to rot."

"Well, look at it this way. If you lie to me, I'll kill you, one hundred per cent guaranteed. Tell me the truth, and who knows what will happen—maybe you'll find a way to survive, and get back to Earth."

A pause.

"How long?"

"Thirty-seven Earth years," he whispers.

I was half-expecting it, but it's still like a punch to the gut. "Thirty-seven?" I say. "Twelve orbits?"

"Something like that."

"So I'm thirty-seven years old?"

"More like forty-seven. I don't know for sure. About the same age as me."

"Explain," I say. "How can I not remember any of this?"

His whole body seems to relax, now the truth is out; the words flow out from him in staccato bursts.

"It's your brain," he says wearily. "They fucked about with your brain, when you were first made. Shoved instruments inside your head, and deliberately damaged part of your brain—your hippocampus, that's what it was called. Stops you from forming long-term memories. Your short-term memory's not affected, and your muscle memory is fine, you can still remember how to walk, drive a jeep, do your shifts. But your long-term memories—they fade away. It's not an exact science, but they reckon you've got around six months' memory before it starts to get hazy."

"The headaches," I say, "that's why our heads ache all the time."

"Yeah. The brain's not an electric circuit. You can't just cut a few wires. There's going to be a bit of collateral fucking damage." He sighs. "Big outcry about it when it all became public, if I remember right. Can't pretend I was out waving placards myself, but... yeah. Big outcry.

"Not that it changed anything. The programme carried on regardless. Money talks, like it always has and always will."

"So, what—we were up on the ships for my first ten years? Doctors meddling about with our brains?"

"Ah…"

"The truth, Ortiz. You might as well, now. It's easier than making up lies."

"Earth, Leila. You were born on Earth. All of you were. There's no way they could get all of the machinery and manpower needed for the programme up into space."

"You're lying. You must be."

A little whistle escapes from his nose, and I realise I'm pressing on his throat too hard, a thin red line springing up under the spike. I relax, and he breathes hard, speaks again.

"Leila. It wasn't me who bought you here. None of this is my idea. I'm no angel—God knows I've done a few bad things in my life—but I didn't do this. And I'm here against my will; I'm a prisoner here too. You see—"

"Yeah, yeah. I've heard all this off the Bees. Don't expect my sympathy. I know what you're here for. How many men did you kill again?"

"And by Earth, I've paid for what I've done."

I take a deep breath, slow my heartbeat down. "Okay. Rewind. Tell me about the programme. What's it about? Why did they grow us, muck about with our brains, and send us out here?"

"Money," he says. "Always money."

"Go on."

He lifts his eyes to the ceiling, and addresses that rather than me. "People had known about these M-Type asteroids for decades. Packed full of metals, enough to solve all our shortages a hundred times over. Only problem—it was mind-bogglingly expensive to send missions there. People came up with all sorts of ideas—robotics, technical wizardry—but they were always just pipedreams. Completely unviable, financially. Then a few bright sparks, at a company called Spiral Systems, came up with an idea. Why not mine the ore the old-fashioned way? Send out humans to do all the dirty work, extracting the ore themselves? The only stumbling block—logistically, financially, you're talking about missions that would last over a decade—two years to get there, seven years on site, two years back. Eleven years stranded on an asteroid? Bugger that! You're not going to be able to find regular people to do that, no matter how much you pay them.

"So they developed the Families programme. Very hush-hush. This all came out years later, when I was a boy. First of all, it was just Ays. Grown and trained in labs on Earth, a few hundred in that first wave. A lot of failures, a lot of problems before they even got them into space. From the brain tampering, especially. God knows how many vegetables they made before they got that right. But eventually, up they went, a mission to deliver them to four asteroids—with a few Overseers to supervise: prisoners like me who were offered a second chance. Then they sat back, and waited for a few years, worked on refining the Families programme.

"And after eleven years, the first Collection ship returned. Two of the asteroids were balls-ups. Everyone dead. Accident, equipment failure, mutiny, who knows.

But two of them worked—the Overseers came back, with the swag. As for the Ays—they stayed out there. After eleven years, they'd long forgotten about Earth."

"But surely," I say, "Spiral could have let them come back, and sent out some new ones?"

"Couldn't have afforded it. You have any idea how much it cost to develop the Families? To send each Ay into space? Spiral had invested billions into every single brother. Just seven years' labour, it didn't pay off. But put them out there, on a loop, orbit after orbit, mining swag—and suddenly it's a different proposition. Long-term investment, but it paid off. Even those two asteroids worth of metal, from seven years' work—suddenly Spiral had more money than God. The ships bought back more fucking metal than they ever thought possible, and all the investors came rushing in. So they started Wave 2— that's you. Not just Ays this time, they'd learnt from the balls-ups before—you've got to have a mixture. So a whole range of brothers and sisters—Bees, Cees, Dees, the lot, all bred for different roles. Some families didn't work out, production lines were discontinued pretty quickly. But the rest of you—just kids, really—off you went. Rumours were going round now about the programme, and there were protests, but I guess they got drowned out by the voices of people who were happy to have metals again. Earth's economy had changed almost overnight.

"And out on the asteroids, thirty-seven years ago, you lot started your life sentences, you poor sods. Every seven years, another Collection ship would head out with a load of ex-con Overseers, to replace the old ones. Plus a load of replacements for the more expendable brothers: mainly Ays and some Jays. The ones most likely to have been damaged, doing all the heavy-duty work."

"Ashton," I breathe.

"Right. He was on the ship with us. A slightly different model from the Wave 2.1 Ays. Andy and Jupiter were replacements too, from previous ships. And when the next Collection Ship comes, you'll get a new Ay to replace Avery.

"So anyway, back on Earth, Spiral's investment was long paid off. All their Families were out on the asteroids, digging away like eager fucking beavers, waiting for their trip to the Promised Land, but never quite getting there. Always in the distance, agonisingly out of reach.

"Then I made a few stupid choices in my life, ended up on death row. Never mind how, but I did. So five years ago, I got the choice: the needle, or a trip out here. I said here, 'cause, well, you've got to, haven't you? Off I went—on a ship with Reynolds, Lee, Fedorchuk. Plus Ashton and dozens of other new Ays. We all felt sorry for you poor bastards, but what could we do about it? If we'd told you the truth, it would've cause a riot, and for what? Spiral sure as hell aren't going to ship you back."

"I bet it was just eating you up inside."

"Look," Ortiz say, "it's a shitty situation, but it is what it is. I'm not your enemy here."

I'm close to tears now. "But this is *slavery!*"

"I know—bastards, right?"

"Oh, no. You're not on my *team*, Ortiz. Not on our side. You don't get that luxury."

"Nah, I wouldn't make that mistake, not when you're this close to cutting my throat. Can you release the pressure a bit? It's getting hard to talk."

I ease the spike back a little, and Mr Ortiz twists his shoulders. He looks uncomfortable. I feel numb, like an out-of-body experience, like it's Leila's body sitting on the Overseer, and I'm watching outside her, in the top corner of the cabin. Already I'm thinking ahead with a dozen questions. Like *Do I tell the Jays?* and *How can I remember this?* and *What's it all got to do with Lily?*

I tell my brain to shut up.

"So let me get this straight," I say. "You've only been here three years?"

"Something like that."

"So there'll be no Collection ship coming for another four years?"

"Afraid not."

"But how does that work? How have you stalled us for more than *thirty years?* How did we not get suspicious?"

"It's not as hard as you'd think. They gave us full instructions before we left, on how to manage you. When your long-term memory only lasts a few months, it's quite easy to keep giving you excuses why there's been a delay. We're behind quota, or there's a problem with the launch of the Collection ship—always re-setting the clock, delaying Collection. You're permanently a year away from going to Earth. Of course, sometimes there have been disputes and revolts, it hasn't always been easy—but gradually, you forget, and we carry on until it's time for another delay."

"The Rota," I say, "you destroy it as you go along."

"'Course we do. There's a permanent archive of around six years for the look of the thing."

That scrap of Rota, then, had been Lily's suspicion. She tore off half a page, to see what would happen to the other half—would it move backwards, disappear? All part of the Curious Case of Time Dilation on Mizushima. But someone was wise to her, and removed the half-page of evidence.

It wasn't the only attempt to exploit our short memories, either. Think of Mr Reynolds, carefully taking turns with the Bees, each one every few months, to keep them from remembering what was going on; but if he thought the Bees wouldn't discuss with each other, he was mistaken.

"And every seven years?" I say. "How does it work when the Collection Ship arrives?"

"The new Overseers come in and announce the existing Overseers are going home in disgrace. Quotas unfulfilled, poor management, etcetera. Spare Ays like Ashton are integrated, and eventually it's forgotten that they're different to the rest."

"And spare Ells?"

"I... no, not as far as I know. They usually just replace any broken Ays or Jays. When we arrived, it was just the two of you here."

"So what really happened to my four sisters?"

"I'm sorry. I just don't know."

I think back to the cabinet. I hadn't seen any mention

of other Ells. Old, forgotten Ays, yes, and notes from old Overseers—but Earth knows what they had destroyed, along with the Rota archive.

"Listen," Ortiz says, a note of desperation creeping into his voice, "we weren't bad Overseers, really. The ones we took over from, they seemed like right bastards. I read the notes they left behind. We've just tried to do the best we could."

I think of Reynolds and the Bees and say nothing.

"Don't kill me, Leila. I know you're angry, but I'm not the one to blame."

"What about Lily? Did you kill her?"

"I swear I didn't. I just want to get home, there's no need for any killing."

"But Lily was on the verge of figuring out what was going on here," I say. "How close she was, we'll never know. But she knew Ashton was different, she had realised something funny was going on with the Rota archive, she knew someone was playing about with our history. She was sticking her nose in, and if she worked it out, this whole fairy tale would have crashed around us, wouldn't it? We'd have become one of the balls-ups. No trip home for Mr Ortiz, no pardon back on Earth."

"Not me. I swear it. I never even spoke to Lily about this. I've said all along, it's the Jays. Leila!"

I'm pressing too hard again, and he coughs, gasps as I ease the pressure.

"So," I say. "What now? You've left me in a difficult situation."

"I don't know what else to say."

"Well, I can't straddle you with a spike to your throat forever, can I?"

"You're not going back to Earth," he says softly. "They'll never let you. Would it be so bad to live out the rest of your days here and forget? You know what they say—ignorance is bliss?"

"Easy for you to say. You've got your ticket back to Earth."

"Earth's not all it's cracked up to be," he says. "You can make things work, here."

"This time next year, I'll have forgotten this conversation, won't I? And what tune will you be singing then, I wonder? How many of us will still be alive?"

I need to talk this over with the Bees and Jays. I can't work out the answer by myself. Together, we could work out a strategy.

But Mr Ortiz decides to take matters into his own hands. I glance to the side, figuring out how to extricate myself from his cabin with minimum awkwardness, and he takes his chance. Quick as a viper, his right hand's free, and he snatches out and grips my wrist. His fingers are cold and rough. He twists my wrist violently, and with a yell I fumble the spike.

He draws himself up to a sitting position, and with his left fist he punches me full in the face. I fall off the cot, nose and eyes smarting, waves of nausea pounding at me. I'm too shocked to cry out.

I scrabble on the floor, but I can barely stand; the bastard hit me as hard as he could. Tears and snot are streaming down my face. In the corner of my eye, I can make out Ortiz, lazily stepping down from the cot, spike in his hand.

"Nothing personal, Leila," he says, pushing me back to the floor with his foot. "Like I said, I think you're in a shitty situation. But there we are. Nothing you or I can do about it. I've still got a chance, though, and I don't plan to die on some shitty fucking asteroid, millions of miles from home."

"Bastard," I manage to hiss.

He frowns, and points the spike at my chest. "I told you the truth, by the way. Whoever killed your sister, it wasn't me. But I'm sorry, girlie—you, I've got to kill."

I close my eyes and wince.

At that moment, there's a *bang* as the door crashes open. I open my eyes and see a Jay running in. Mr Ortiz swivels, swears, raises the spike—

And the Jay points a taser at him (of course the Jays stole the taser—how could I have doubted it?) and twin wires shoot out, landing right in Ortiz's chest. There's a buzz, and Ortiz convulses as he falls to the floor. His arms and legs continue to twitch, and I have to look away. It's creepy.

The Jay ambles towards me, steps over the stricken body, and offers me a hand.

"Jeremy," he says. I take his hand, still dizzy, and he pulls me up. "I'm sure you had everything under control. But I just wanted to lend a hand."

"Were you listening?" I say.

"Of course. Heard you heading up the spine, so I followed to keep an eye on you. Then I was listening by the door while you thrashed it out with Ortiz. Well played, by the way."

"Yeah. Any time. You too—thanks for saving my life and everything."

"So."

"So. Pretty crazy, right? Now what?"

Ortiz is stirring. A little bit of spittle forms at his lips.

"I think you need to leave for a few minutes," he says, fingering the spike. "We can't let him live, Leila."

"All right," I say. I reach out and pluck the taser from his hands. "Mr Lee's mine, though. And I don't need any help with that."

"All right," he says, after a pause. "Then we regroup in the Leisure cabin and decide what to do next. Okay?"

I nod, stumble out, and abandon Mr Ortiz to his fate.

19

REVOLUTION

WE SUIT UP in silence. Mr Lee is watching me, but I refuse to meet his eyes. In the corner of the airlock, a red light flashes lazily. I count the beats between the flashes. One... two... three... four—

Flash.

I fix my hood on, taking my time, letting Mr Lee sweat it out.

I'd told him I'd found some new clues, in the tunnel where Lily died. He was wary, wanted to know more details, but I was firm, saying he needed to see the clues *in situ*. I suggested that I show Mr Ortiz, if he didn't want to come, and that made him change his tune—soon he was following me to the airlock, no arguments.

"Ready?" he asks.

We step outside and board Banana, the last remaining jeep. I let him drive, out of spite. He doesn't have much of a feel for the pedals, and Banana jerks back and forth as we make our way to the East tunnel complex. He's gripping the wheel tight, as if he could snap it. His channel patches into mine.

"*Why don't you tell me what these clues are?*" he says. "*Better than trying to have a conversation at the bottom of a mineshaft.*"

"I'd prefer to do it my way, Mr Lee," I say. "Trust me."

"*I do trust you, but there's no need to be theatrical, Leila.*"

"Mmm."

"*You're not trying to do a Poirot, are you?*" he says, trying and failing to inject a light-hearted note into his voice.

"It's Marple," I say. "I prefer Marple. Just be patient. All will be revealed when we get inside the tunnel."

I'm trying to think of all the ramifications of what Mr Ortiz told me, but I don't know where to start. As we pass the rim of a crater, it suddenly hits me that I'm *old*. I'm not a child, fresh out the vats, I'm forty-five, I'm *ancient*. All those orbits, plugging away in the depots... Earth! How many more cycles have I got left in me, anyway?

As I gaze out of Banana, peering up at the stars, the sheer bloody unfairness of it all hits me. I mean, really, it's too much. All those millions of people on Earth, they all knew, they all *allowed* this to happen. Somehow, I could have accepted it if they'd dropped the pretence, if it was admitted that this was a slave colony. But the bloody bastards didn't even have the courage to do that. So they set up this farce. Why? To protect our feelings, or theirs?

We hit a bump and both jerk forward. Mr Lee is tapping his foot, shaking it practically. He patches in and mutters something about dust and visibility.

As for you, I think. *As for you, you lying worm....*

For a moment, I consider how satisfying it would be to barge him, grab the wheel, and send the jeep tumbling down the dunes. The urge is almost overwhelming; I have to fight it down. At least with the people of Earth, all they did was close their eyes and turn away. Easy enough to do, when you can't see the person you've condemned to a life of servitude. But Mr Lee—

How many times has he looked me in the eyes and lied to my face? He was the only person on Hell I really trusted, apart from Lily. When he lied about death row, I was angry, but I kind of understood—it was his story, his life. But this—this is on a whole new level. Every time he spoke to me, it was a lie; every time he kept silent, it was a betrayal. And then there are the Overseers before him, who I can't remember. Every single one—thirty-seven years of lies.

He's the worst of them all, though—with his smiles, and his poxy books, and his gentle, avuncular manner— like he's not an Overseer, we're friends really, like this whole business of *ore mining* demeaned us both. And the whole time, he was laughing at me. At least Mr Ortiz and Mr Reynolds were honest about what they thought of us.

I want to be sick. I want to replay every conversation I've ever had, everything I've ever seen. So many lies—his insinuations about Mr Fedorchuk and the Jays; the fantasies he painted for me about what life on Earth would be like. I want to go back and rip out every memory I've ever had of him—make it all un-happen.

Mr Lee: sad face, comforting me after Lily's funeral. Mr Lee: concerned face, advising me about my investigations and warning me about the Jays. Mr Lee: patient face, giving me a hand and packing ore in the depot. Good Earth, I want to smash something.

You smiling sack of shit, I think. *You poxing liar.*

And he will say it was to protect us, but the truth matters, it really does. The truth of what we're doing here is all we have. Because once you pull away the curtain—the fantasy of vats and targets, the reward of a journey to Earth—once that is gone, the smallness of the truth, the banality of it, is just so pathetic that I feel my whole body shrinking in on itself. I mean, what are you left with, when that's all gone? Twenty brothers and sisters, trudging to and from the mines, cycle after cycle, orbit after orbit. An eternity of swag piling up and up, filling the depot. No wonder the Overseers despise us.

WE REACH THE tunnel complex, and Mr Lee turns off the engine. "*Lead on, then, Leila,*" he says.

We climb out, and I pass the spot where I saw Jolly cradling my sister's body. I head for the tunnel entrance, with a last look up at the watery sun, now at its zenith. Then into the mineshaft where Jolly said he found her body. Eighteen cycles ago, she came here with her killer.

I step back and gesture to Mr Lee. "You go first," I say, patching in. "Keep going until I tell you to stop."

He stops for a second. Darts a quick look at me, then presses forward. "*The anticipation is killing me, Leila.*"

After a few steps, he has to crouch down, and I follow him in. He leaves the trolley for me, and shuffles along at a slow pace. I take the rope and pull myself along, pausing occasionally to let him get ahead. Soon he's on his hands and knees, crawling along down the track. After a hundred feet I call a halt.

"Far enough," I say.

"*Where's the evidence, Leila? I don't see anything.*"

"Never mind the evidence."

Something in my voice makes him look over his shoulder. I'm pointing the taser at him, at the small of his back.

"*What's going on, Leila?*" he says, with a kind of forced, strained calm.

"I had a little chat with Mr Ortiz," I say. "He told me everything."

"*What do you mean?*"

He starts to manoeuvre around to face me, and I bark, "Hold it!" He freezes, and slowly turns back to the depths of the mineshaft.

"How we've been here rather longer than the six years we believed. How there's going to be no collection for us, not ever. How Spiral Systems shipped us here from Earth, for a lifetime of slavery. How you've been lying to us every minute of every cycle that I've known you."

To his credit, he does not try to bluster. "*Okay,*" he says.

"Okay? *Okay?* That's your response?"

"*I don't know what else to say.*"

"No moral relativism? No shifting the blame onto Spiral? No, um, apology?"

"*I'm truly sorry. Truly. But I don't think an apology is the slightest bit good enough. My only defence—what would you have me do differently? Should I have told you the truth?*"

"You said something similar when I found out about your past," I say bitterly.

"*And I was right, just like I am now. What good would it have done?*"

"I'm not going to argue the rights and wrongs of that. What I've brought you here for is Lily."

"*Lily?*"

"You killed her, didn't you? She was close to figuring it all out. This whole sordid little conspiracy. And she came to you with questions, because she trusted you. But you couldn't let her find out, could you? You had to return to Earth. Had to see your family again. So, Lily had to be silenced."

Over the channel, I can hear Mr Lee's long, tired sigh.

"*Leila...*"

"Andrew saw you outside the tunnels. A grey-stripe suit. I thought it was Mr Reynolds, but the Bees were with him the whole time. How did you get her there in the jeep? Did you tell her you were going to show her something that would explain away all her concerns?

"Regardless, after you'd killed her, and hidden her body deep in the tunnel, you drove straight to the depot, to try and find the evidence she had told you about. I'm right, aren't I? Because there were only two people she might have spoken to about her three clues—you, or Juan. But Juan was with me in East 3. He could have killed Lily, but he didn't have a jeep to take to the depot."

"*It was an act of mercy.*"

"Mercy? Really?"

"*Look at your lives, Leila!*" he spits, making me jump. "*You're stuck in a loop you can't escape. But at least you're not forced to* acknowledge *it. What good does it do to know the truth?*"

"I—"

"*Lily guessed, but I saved her from finding out the whole, grim reality. That's what I did, it was the very least I could do.*"

Tears are welling up, I can hardly see through the visor.

"And me too? That's why you sabotaged my jeep? Another 'act of mercy'?"

"*It was just supposed to give you a scare!*" he shouts. "*To warn you off! Please, Leila, try to understand!*"

"You're running out of lies. You know I'm too stubborn to be warned off."

"*Ortiz should never have told you. Whatever you did to him, he should never have told you.*"

"How did you kill her? Did you look her in the eye when you did it? Did you?"

"*I made it as quick and painless as I could.*"

"You've lied to me this whole time, you're lying to me now. An act of mercy! You killed her 'cause you were scared! You just wanted to get home!"

"*I still have a life! You want me to throw mine away, because you can't have one?*"

I shudder. A horrible thought strikes me. The four other Ells I dreamed of: Lolita, Lilith, Lara, Lucia. They were *real*—it wasn't a fantasy.

And with complete certainty, I know they didn't die up in a spaceship, but that we were once a Family of Ells on Hell, all six of us. Half-formed pictures now, echoes of my last conversation with Lily in our cabin. *Something stinks here, Lei, you know it does.*

Images, sounds, fill my brain. I have a clear memory of four Ells in our cabin, whispering, something that didn't make sense—one of my sisters saying she was going to... investigate. And another image that flashes past: Mr Lee, me and another Ell, but it's not Lily, I could swear to that. There was a third Ell here, then, alive as recently as the last orbit.

"Has this happened before?" I ask him. "Did you kill my other sisters when they started to investigate? Am I just the last one to figure it out?"

"*No! I swear to you! There were just two of you when I arrived—I don't know what happened to the other four.*"

"You're lying."

"*Leila, I'm not a killer like Ortiz. Lily was... I panicked. I couldn't persuade her to show me the clues she had found, or tell me where she had hidden them—we started to argue. I think she realised that I was part of the conspiracy, that she shouldn't have confided in me. She started to head back to the jeep. Everything was going to come crashing down—I panicked.*"

"I thought it was an act of mercy."

His sobs come crackling over the channel. "*I'm sorry, Leila. I never—*"

I cut off the patch. I don't want to hear any more. I wasn't sure up 'til this moment, what I was going to do. But this is the final betrayal. It's not enough that they imprisoned us here on this lump of rock, not enough that they set us to an unwitting lifetime of labour. They had to kill all five of my sisters, because the Ells couldn't help investigating, they'd worked out something was rotten on Hell. And so, in the horrible words of Mr Ortiz, our production line was 'discontinued.' No need to bring out replacements for the pesky Ells who were stirring the pot, and sticking their noses into the inner workings of Hell. Just kill them off, one by one.

And that is too much to bear.

I pull the trigger on the taser and it whips out with a flash, takings him in the back. His legs spasm and he collapses to the floor, shuddering. Then I take a sharp lump of swag, and smash it down on the tube connecting his oxygen supply. I twist it, making a small rip, which thrashes as the oxygen escapes. I don't know how long he'll be unconscious for, but he won't have enough oxygen to walk all the way back to base.

Let him spend his last minutes knowing he's about to die. It's more than he gave Lily.

I turn around awkwardly in the mineshaft and a shower of ore dust falls on my hood. I shuffle out, suddenly exhausted. The Overseers are gone. The revolution has happened, almost by accident.

The Ays won't like it—but they'll have to go along with it, once they see where the wind has blown. I straighten up as the tunnel opens to the mouth of the warren—the 'lobby,' as Mr Lee used to call it. Sunlight is streaming in, reflecting off the quartz, and it's sparkling, so damn beautiful that for a moment I forget about everything.

EPILOGUE

A NEW DAWN

MY EYES SNAP open. For a few seconds, I have that thrilling, terrifying sensation of not knowing where I am or who I am. Then I turn my head to the side, see Jeremy, asleep, and I remember again.

I have a work shift commencing in forty-seven minutes. We are mining as much swag as we can, but it is a struggle. With only ten of us left on the asteroid, ore yield is grinding to a halt. Four Bees, three Jays, two Ays. And one Ell, me, poor little Leila. It would help, of course, to have the Overseers back, but they are buried deep in the bowels of Hell. I can remember their names—Ortiz, Lee, Reynolds, Fedorchuk—but not their faces. Mr Lee—sometimes I feel like I can picture him, but then the image will drift away.

The Jays have taken on most the Overseers' responsibilities, and keep all their papers locked in one of the cabinets. Joseph manages the Rota as best he can. The two remaining Ays, Andrew and Aaron, have to endure a punishing schedule, and whenever I see them, they are lying exhausted in one of the Communal cabins—broken men.

I get to my feet, carefully moving Jeremy's arm, not waking him. I walk to the mirror. A lined face stares back at me, crow's feet crawling out the eye sockets. I think of my five sisters—Lily and the other four. It seems unfair that our Family was the only one to be reduced like this, but I get on with it. I have Jeremy to keep me company, at least. The hardest thing for me to bear is surviving without books. The reader broke many cycles ago—the screen just gave up, now a dead, grey rectangle. And with that, my portal to Earth disappeared too—all those stories, all those lives. I can still recall traces of some of the more memorable stories. *And Then There Were None*, with the ten strangers stuck on an island: that strikes a chord. Or *Brave New World*, with its alphas and betas and gammas—all written over a century before the Families existed.

Sometimes, I'll whisper the stories to myself in my cot, or what I can remember of them, when Jeremy's asleep.

I wash my face and get dressed. Everything seems slower these cycles, like moving through treacle. And my body aches all over, surely more than it used to. I can feel twinges in both knees, a dull ache in my back, a constant headache, a pain in my gut, a long scar down my leg that flares up at night and stops me from sleeping. Jeremy occasionally lets me take the pills, and they help to dull the pain.

In his cot, he stirs. He finds this cabin too big and empty, and it disrupts his sleep. It was an Overseer's cabin once—Mr Ortiz, I think, though I can't be sure. Sometimes he'll retreat to the old Jays' cabin, but he always ends up coming back. He won the cabin in a chess game, and I think he's determined to enjoy his prize.

I DRIVE TO the Depots in Cabbage, alone. Everywhere always seems so quiet and empty now, with just ten of us. I mean, I'm not saying we were permanently bumping into each other before, or having traffic jams—but you'd see someone in the spine and say hello, or walk into the Community cabin and have a chat with a couple of brothers. Even in the tunnels, just having another body a few hundred metres away would be a comfort. Whereas now, driving across the plains of Hell, or loading swag onto a trailer, you feel like you could be the last person left in the universe.

I climb out of the jeep, wander into the ore depot. It's a dismal sight. Crates of swag are dumped in a sprawling mess, with black rocks spilling out from every one. The Ays would be horrified if they saw. There's no order, none of the regularity I see in the rows of crates towards the back of the depot. Really, I have no idea what I'm doing here. What I wouldn't give to have Mr Lee back, or a couple of my sisters. Together, we'd get things back on track.

As I walk up the rows, I realise tears are springing to my eyes, and I'm not sure why.

ACCORDING TO JOLLY, the Collection Ship is due to arrive in around 500 cycles. I just hope we'll have collected enough.

ACKNOWLEDGEMENTS

Many thanks to beta readers Chris Dugan and Ben Geiger, to David Moore and all the team at Abaddon, and to Jennie Goloboy for taking a chance on me and being such a splendid agent. Also, there would be no book without my wife Nicki, who has encouraged my writing for so long, or my Mum and Dad, who tolerated my obsessive reading habits (especially of Agatha Christie) when I was a boy.

ABOUT THE AUTHOR

Alex Thomson is a French and Spanish teacher from Letchworth Garden City. This is his debut novel, though his short fiction has been published in the *Nocturne* anthologies. He wrote *Death of a Clone* on the train during his daily commute to London, scribbling away in biro in a notebook, surrounded by sweaty commuters.

FIND US ONLINE!

www.rebellionpublishing.com

/rebellionpub /rebellionpublishing /rebellionpub

SIGN UP TO OUR NEWSLETTER!

rebellionpublishing.com/sign-up

YOUR REVIEWS MATTER!

Enjoy this book? Got something to say?

Leave a review on Amazon, GoodReads or with your
favourite bookseller and let the world know!

FIND US ONLINE!

www.rebellionpublishing.com

@rebellion   /rebellionpublishing   /rebellion

SIGN UP TO OUR NEWSLETTER!

rebellionpublishing.com/sign-up

YOUR REVIEWS MATTER!